TARTARUS

IVY COLE

TW - This book contains mentions of blood and guns. PTSD trigger warning of torture, abuse, rape, and mentions of rape. This is your warning. Please be advised.

To my readers:

Thank you so much for your constant support and for reading the books
that I pour my heart and soul into.
P.S. I'm sorry for what I'm about to do, please don't throw the book across
the room!

To my Alpha and Beta readers:

Don't tell them a damn thing, you know you loved every bit of it! You
wanted to kill him too!

To those who have ADHD:

May our squirrels and ducks never be in a row and bathe in the utter chaos!
We will eventually figure out where the music is coming from, until then
let's party! I'll bring the glow sticks!

CONTENTS

Also By

CHAPTER ONE
MACY

Six years old...

I stand staring at the door, waiting. Mommy will come back. She always does. But it's getting late, and she's always home before the pretty colors in the sky turn dark. I hear Daddy banging around in the kitchen. He was angry when he got home. I jump when I hear him yell from the kitchen.

"Come on! Let's eat."

"But what about Mommy?"

"She won't be back, munchkin. Close the door, and let's eat."

Frowning, I do as I'm told. Walking into the kitchen, I see Daddy drinking from one of the bottles he says are only for adults. They must taste good because he's had a lot since he got home. Climbing into the chair, I look up at him and ask, "What do you mean Mommy isn't coming back? She always comes back."

He slams his fist on the table, and I cringe. He runs the same hand through his hair. "Sorry, munchkin," he says with a sigh, "Mommy left us. It's just you and me now."

My lip trembles when I see the tears in his eyes. Something bad happened. "What happened to Mommy?"

He pulls away from the table and kneels down in front of me. He tucks some of my wavy brown hair behind my ear, then he cups my face. "Mommy didn't want to stay with Daddy anymore."

"But... why did she leave me, too?"

He presses a kiss against my forehead. "I don't know, munchkin. But I'll love you enough for the both of us, alright?" He pulls me into his arms, hugging me tightly.

That night, my little six-year-old self learned something about love. Love is optional. Love can fade until there isn't there's nothing left. The true love in my children's shows doesn't exist in real life. It is a fairytale.

Ten years later...

I let out a sigh and get back to scrubbing the floor. I hate cleaning up throw-up. Dad comes home drunk more often than not these days. A few years ago, he also began taking drugs. Apparently, the pain of my mother leaving broke something in him. He's also started gambling, which is where most of our money goes.

If I wanted to eat, I had to learn how to steal and get creative in coming up with ways to get free food. I go down to the homeless shelter a few times a week, and I've learned who will look past a teenager walking in and who will gladly call Child Protective Services.

Thank god this piece of shit house is paid off because we couldn't afford the payments. I'm lucky if I can get money from my dad to pay for the utilities. The electricity has gone out a few times, but it's only in the winter that Dad will make sure to give me enough money to pay the gas bill.

As much as I hate how we're living, I would never leave Dad alone. He's the one who stayed. He didn't leave me like Mom did. He's also the only one I can talk to. No one at school wants to be my friend. They say I'm too poor and that I have a deadbeat dad. I punched the girl who said that in the face. They suspended me for a few days, but I haven't had a problem with her since, so that's a plus.

Throwing the scrubber into the basin of water, I sit up on my heels and stretch my arms over my head. I jump up from the floor when the front door slams open. When I see that it's my dad, I relax. He's blurry-eyed, so he's been drinking. With a sigh, I make my way over to him. "You need help?"

He waves a hand erratically in the air. "I'm all good. I made money at the casino today!"

I try not to get excited because I know exactly where the money will end up. "Oh, did you? That's great."

He pats me on the head. "It's more than great! I can use it to make even more money!" He grabs my hands and starts spinning me around, and I can't help but laugh. He grins and says, "We are going to make it out of here, munchkin! Just you wait. Life will be amazing for us."

His words seem so genuine, and I want to believe him so badly. I play along and ask, "Where are we going to go, Dad?"

He stops spinning. "Anywhere, munchkin! We can go to the mountains or the beach. We can even go to another country!" He loses his footing, but I catch him before he falls. He smiles up at me. "Always there when I need you, munchkin."

I smile sadly down at him. "Of course, Dad."

He steadies himself and wraps me in his arms. "I love you so much, little munchkin."

I hold him back just as tight. "I love you too, Dad." And I do. He's the only one who loves me. The only person I can trust not to stab me in the back. All the girls and boys at school laugh at me. They pretend to be my friends and then pull pranks to humiliate me in front of the entire school. But that's fine. I don't need them. I don't need anyone else. Only my dad. The only person I can trust.

CHAPTER TWO
MACY

Two years later...

Finally! I'm eighteen. I graduated with a 3.0., which I have to say is impressive considering how much I had to fight to even get that. It's a good enough grade point average that most colleges will at least consider me. I'll finally be able to leave this shithole of a town. Dad has gone downhill since he won at the casino two years ago. He lost it all and has been trying to win it back ever since.

He's only worsened his debt, though, and I've had to do my best to pay it off. Most of the money was from a part-time job I was able to get from the old lady down the street. I did odd jobs around her house, mowed the grass, and shoveled the snow in the winter. She paid me more than I thought she should, but I think she felt bad for me.

Dad didn't make it to my graduation, which I have to admit hurts a lot. I've stuck by his side through everything. The least he could do was show up at my graduation and cheer for me. Instead, I had to suffer through looks of pity and the popular girls snickering as I left the center and caught a bus home.

Sighing, I lie down on my unmade, ratty bedspread. I look up at the ceiling and wonder what my life will be like once I escape this place. As much as I don't want to leave Dad behind, I need to make something of myself. If I don't go now, I'll be stuck here forever.

There's a bang on the door downstairs, and I groan. Fuck! I bet it's another debt collector or one of Dad's drug dealers. As I make my way down the stairs, there's another bang on the door. "Fuck, I'm coming. Hold on a damn second!" The moment I open the door, I regret it. It's fucking Marvin. He is creepy as fuck and has had an eye on me since I turned sixteen. Dad doesn't seem to notice, but I catch the looks he gives me. He wants me as one of his call girls.

I put my foot behind the open door, hoping to prevent him from barging in as I sneer. "What do you want, Marvin?"

He licks his lips as he looks me over. "You've filled out so well, little Macy."

I try not to vomit in my mouth. "What do you want?" I repeat.

He grins. "I'm here for the money your dad owes me."

"How much does he owe?"

He leans an elbow against the door frame. Then, leaning in close, he says, "Four grand."

Four grand!! How the fuck does my dad owe that much money? I certainly don't have that type of money in reserve. "He doesn't have the money right now."

Marvin smiles. "I've allowed him to put a hold on the amount for too long. I need my money by tonight."

"He won't be able to get you the money by then."

He looks me up and down again. "Then it seems he will have to pay off his debt in another way."

I growl and spit out, "I'll make sure you get the money tonight."

"See that you do, Macy."

I slam the door in his face, but I can hear his chuckle as he walks down the stairs and back to his car. Fuck! How the hell am I going to get four grand? I'm pacing the living room when the door opens, and I look over to find Dad. He's drunk and also high. His widened pupils and bloodshot eyes are what tip me off.

He looks at me for a moment as if trying to focus on me. Finally, he smiles, "What's wrong, munchkin?"

I sigh. "Marvin was here. He wants his money tonight."

He blows out a raspberry. "It will be fine. I've got everything under control."

I arch a brow. "Really?"

He nods as he makes his way over to the couch. Falling onto it, he pulls out his phone. He stares at the screen for a moment and then squints. I watch as he scrolls down a list of names. Finally, he presses on a name and puts the phone to his ear. "Hey, Marv!"

I can only hear Dad's side of the conversation, and all he keeps doing is nodding. As if Marvin can see him. Then he says, "Of course! Come on over." He hangs up the phone and smiles up at me. "All good."

I frown. "I'm sure it's not that easy, Dad. What did he want?"

Dad shrugs. "He only wanted some collateral."

I freeze. "Collateral?"

"Yeah."

Biting my lip, I ask, "Did he say what he wanted as collateral?"

He waves a hand in the air. "He said we would discuss it when he got here. It'll be fine."

I have severe doubts about that, but before I can voice them, there is a knock at the door. Damn, that was quick. Reluctantly, I walk to the front door and open it. Marvin is on the other side, and he's smiling widely at me. Fuck.

He walks in without invitation. "Liam! So good to see you."

My dad pushes himself off the couch and smiles at Marvin. "Hey, Marv!"

They shake hands, and Marvin wraps an arm around my dad's shoulder. "So, we were going to discuss collateral."

Dad nods. "Of course! I'll be able to get your money by the end of the week."

Marvin pats his shoulder. "Of course, you will."

I look into Marvin's eyes, and I can see his utter glee over the collateral he is going to ask for. Because we both know my father isn't going to come up with that money.

"Well, I figure your beautiful daughter could keep me company while you work to get my money for me."

I see the surprise flare in my father's eyes, but he nods. "It shouldn't take me too long to get the money. I'm sure she wouldn't mind."

I stand, my eyes wide and mouth agape. Is my father so high and drunk that he doesn't realize what he is allowing to happen? "Dad," I hiss.

He looks over at me with a smile. "It won't take too long, munchkin. It's only for a little while. I promise."

I shake my head. "I am not going with him. You can't make me."

My dad's brows knit together. "It won't be for very long. You would be helping me out, munchkin. Marvin is a nice guy."

Marvin is a piece of shit, but apparently, when the man gives you drugs, you don't ask too many questions. "Dad! Don't make me go with this guy."

Marvin's tone is mocking as he makes a tutting sound and says, "Liam, if she doesn't want to come, I can't promise you any leeway for the money."

Dad's eyes meet mine. "It will only be for a few days, munchkin. Help me out."

Biting my lip, I see that I don't have much of a choice right now. Either Marvin's men shoot my dad in the head due to not paying up, or I give myself over to the man I hate most. Sighing, I resign myself. "Fine."

Marvin's eyes brighten. "Good! Now I'll keep your daughter safe while you pay off your debt, Liam."

My dad nods and smiles at me. "Thanks, munchkin."

I give him a sad smile. "Anything for you, Dad."

Marvin steps up next to me and whispers in my ear, "You're going to be so fun to break, little doll."

I sneer up at him. "In your dreams."

He snickers as he leaves the house, and I follow behind.

I didn't realize it, but my dad never paid off his debt. The only person I have ever trusted gave me up to keep himself debt free because as long as I was with Marvin, he no longer owed him money. That moment was the last time I trusted someone. That was the day I vowed to fight with everything I had for my freedom.

CHAPTER THREE
MACY

Five years later...

"**F**uck off, Marvin!" I yell as I slam my finger down on the end-call button. Just another day of dealing with his bullshit. I'm currently the most highly sought after escort in the Underground, which is great for business and would be even better if I got to keep the money. But all the money I make goes directly to Marvin. He says it's to cover what my dad keeps borrowing and never pays back.

This territory has changed a lot since the Steepe brothers barged into the Underground. A few years ago, they bought out most of the larger companies in the area. They quickly took over the bad habits of the Underground as well. You won't hear any complaints from the Underground, either. I heard the oldest brother was killed in a fight over territory a few years ago. The gang who killed him went silent, and no one has heard anything about them since.

The drug dealers have it made because they get to keep most of the money they make as long as the drugs stay local. Due to the Underworld's leniency towards the lighter drugs like marijuana, drug dealers are making a substantial profit. The brothers don't allow many of the harder drugs in their territory. Most of their money is made from alcohol and prostitution. The girls around here won't complain, though, because we make bank. We get to pick the Johns we deal with, and we split the money 80/20. Our pimps are required to provide us shelter and money for food.

As I said, I *would* be making bank if I could keep any of the money I made. I try to find wealthier Johns and even a few Janes if the money is good enough. I'm not picky. I'm a woman. I know exactly how to pleasure a woman if needed. I steal from them if they are drunk enough. What? Some of them are entitled assholes. If they're not willing to spread the wealth, I'll take some for myself.

There are two things I love to buy with the stolen money, lingerie and fancy dresses. For my John tonight, I picked out my favorite lingerie. I have a few sets that were gifted to me, but I only wear those if I do a repeat John. The pair I'm wearing tonight is a deep blue with diamond jewels that attach to the fabric across my hips and run across my abdomen. The bra is the same color with a lace pattern. The rhinestones attach at the bottom of the cups and run over the curves of my breasts to connect to the straps over my shoulder.

After slipping into the luxurious set, I pull out the dress the John requested I wear for the charity event this evening. I find it funny that guys don't want to show up to these events empty armed, but the women will proudly show up alone.

The dress he requested is a navy blue silk maxi dress with a low-cut v-neck. Sexy but not too sexy. Those were his exact words. The rhinestones peek out from the edges of the v-neck, and I grin. He won't be able to concentrate with those peeking out seductively like that. I'll be able to steal money off of him easily. It will be as easy as taking candy from a baby, as the saying goes. Though diamonds and jewels are so much better than a lollipop. Wouldn't you agree? I suppose the males I take the candy from are about as independent as a baby. Relying on their money and status to get through the world. Anyhow, we are going to a charity event tonight, and what the John doesn't realize is that he will be donating to the broke-ass Macy fund.

I pull out my classic black Louboutin heels. I love these fucking shoes. Nothing says money like a pair of Louboutin's. If the John ever asks if they can buy me something, I always say shoes. Shoes are easily my kryptonite. I have way too many.

Slipping the heels on my feet, I take one last look at myself in the mirror. My eyes are smoky, but it makes my hazel-green eyes pop. Last thing to do is twist my hair up into a chignon before pulling a few strands out to frame my face. Just as I'm finishing, there's a knock at the door. Perfect timing. I grab my purse and look through the peephole. With a smile, I pull the door open. "Evening, Remington."

His warm, wrinkled face smiles down at me. "Evening, Miss. There's a gentleman in the lobby who says he's here to pick you up for the night."

"Yes. Thank you, Rem. You know you didn't have to come all this way. You do have my number."

He nods, offering an elbow. "I know, Miss Macy. But I hate seeing all these men requesting your services. If you were my daughter, I would snatch you out of Marvin's grasp. I would send you far away. You have so much potential."

I smile at the doorman. I absolutely adore this man. He's like the grandpa I never had. I give him a peck on the cheek and say, "Thank you for looking out for me. But this is where I'm stuck until I can find a way out."

His cheeks redden as we make our way into the elevator. "Be safe tonight, Miss Macy."

"I'm always safe," I reply. The door squeals open, and I'm greeted by the gentleman who bought me for the evening. He's your typical handsome, rich man. Brushed-back salt and pepper hair to look distinguished. Classic good looks, but nothing that stands out as special. Just your typical guy buying a night with me to look good in front of all his friends.

He smiles at me as I make my way over to him. He reaches out and kisses the back of my hand. I do the predictable girlish giggle to feed his male ego. "Good evening, Miss Lowell."

I smile shyly. I changed my last name the moment I realized Dad wasn't going to break me out of this life, and I needed to make a name for myself. Macy Lowell. I think it is hilarious that my last name means wolf cub considering who runs the Underground.

He slides my hand into the crook of his elbow, and he ushers me out the front door. He opens the door to his town car for me, and I slide inside. I'm greeted with a roomy interior and a bottle of champagne on ice. Nice. He slides in beside me, leans forward, and taps on the barrier between the driver and us.

"You look beautiful this evening."

I bat my eyes at him. "Thank you very much, Mr. Carmichael."

He slides a hand over my thigh, squeezing softly. "You can call me Warren."

I titter softly. "Well, then you must call me Macy."

He presses his lips to the base of my neck and whispers, "Macy. I hope you have a wonderful time tonight."

I place my hand on his thigh and slide it upward till my pinky grazes the bulge in his pants. "I'm sure I will, Warren."

I've become a master at foreplay and sex. Although, it's rare that I actually enjoy myself. It's hard to find something fun and freeing when it's your job. But I know how to fake it like a champ. Guys don't notice. If you work your internal muscles enough, you can clamp down hard, making them think you had the best orgasm of your entire life. And most of the guys I service don't care much about my pleasure as long as I say the right thing. If they are satisfied, I get more money when I stroke their ego. Also, I started doing this at eighteen. I grew numb for a while before I realized this was going to be my life till I could escape, whenever that may be, so I needed to make it look good.

He sucks in a breath against my neck, nipping my skin and pulling away with a grin. "We have to arrive on time. We will save the fun for after the event."

I fake a pout. "If we must."

He chuckles. "So eager. I'll make sure you're satisfied by the end of the night."

I stifle the eye roll and nod instead. Looking out the window, I stare at the city as we pass, giving myself the same mental pep talk I do before every night out with a John.

You are not a whore. You are doing this to stay alive. You're doing this to save your father's life. You are fighting back the only way you can. You are doing this to survive. Only trust those who prove their worth. Love is for those who can afford a broken heart.

I don't know why I still fight so hard for my dad, but it seems to be the only thing that gets me out of bed each day. Even though he's proven I can't trust him, the love I feel for him has me in a chokehold. I can't let go. I can't walk away. Not yet.

CHAPTER FOUR
MACY

We pull up to the front of a mansion, and the driver parks and jumps out to open the door. Warren slides out, then offers me his hand. I slide mine into his waiting one. He helps me maneuver out the car, and I'm immediately bombarded with flashing lights and people yelling, "Mr. Carmichael!"

Seems the guy is more popular than I initially thought. He slips my hand into the crook of his elbow, then turns and waves to the reporters. I smile shyly as they take pictures. Nothing like publicity to show that the wealthy are charitable people. I'm jerked out of my rambling thoughts when I hear someone yell, "The Steepe brothers have arrived!"

Looking over my shoulder, I see a driver opening the door to a limo. I'm pretty sure I stop breathing when the first brother slips out of the car. I've never met the men who run the Underground, but I've heard a lot about them. The whispers of what they look like didn't do them justice.

The first brother is dressed in a white button-up with black slacks. His black hair is slicked back with a few wisps falling into his eyes. The sides of his head are shaved down, only having a bit of fuzz. I can see a tattoo peeking out from the top of his buttoned-up shirt and his ears have large black gauges. Someone screams, "Silas!" His dark eyes roam the crowd and meet mine briefly. He gives me a curt nod before walking up and past me into the mansion.

My head whips back around when 'Jax' is screamed. The next brother to emerge is large. He looks like a fighter. I can see tattoos across his fingers and hands as he lights a cigarette. His hair, a dark blond color, hits him mid-chest in waves. He winks at the reporters as he pulls it up into a messy bun. Wisps fall out and around his face. I notice that the sides of his head are trimmed short and seem to be a dark brown, almost black color. He blows smoke out his nostrils. Although he doesn't have a beard, his chiseled face is adorned with a five o'clock shadow. He's wearing a black button-up with gray slacks. His gray suit jacket is wide open, letting everyone see that a few of his buttons are undone, showing off his tanned body. He ignores me completely as he walks past me and into the mansion.

I feel Warren tugging on my arm, but I can't help but look to see the last brother.

"Luka!"

He is undeniably the youngest and smallest of the brothers, but he is still muscular and handsome. His look is a mix of the boy next door and a mob boss. He's in a simple black shirt with a black leather jacket and a pair of dark-washed jeans. He gives a roguish smile to the reporters as he passes them. His stubbled jaw not hiding the slight dimples that flash with his smile. His dark brown hair is messily brushed back on top as if he has run his fingers through it several times.

"Sweetheart," Warren hisses beside me. "You're making me look bad. We need to get inside."

Well fuck! I better put on a show or else I won't be getting paid much tonight. I do my best doe eyed impression and say, "Oh my! I'm so sorry, Warren." I run my hand up his arm. "I've only heard about the Steepe brothers. Forgive my curiosity."

He seems to measure if I mean it or not, but something in my eyes must settle him. He nods, ushering me in through the mansion doors.

As we make our way around the room, he introduces me to all his high-end friends. They smile and nod at me politely, but I know they know exactly who I am. I've escorted most of the rich people here. But that would look bad for their image, so they continue to act like they don't know who I am and what I do.

We are halted, and my mouth gapes open before I can stop it. The middle brother, Jax, smiles down at Warren. "Hello, friend. How are you this evening?"

I school my features as quickly as I can before either of them notices. I smile prettily as Warren grins and replies, "I'm doing well this evening. And you?"

Jax shrugs. "Can't complain. Will we see you at the casinos soon?"

Warren nods. "I'll stop by later this week."

I just barely hold back the snort I want to make. Of course these guys would ignore the woman in this conversation. I wonder what kind of food they have here. I hope they have those tiny finger sandwiches. Those are fucking delicious! Oh, maybe they have fancy champagne too. I startle out of my thoughts when I hear my name. "Forgive me," I make myself giggle, pretending to be an airhead who's only a pretty face.

Warren smiles down at me. "I was introducing you to Jax, sweetheart."

I glance up at him and smile. "It's a pleasure."

Jax smirks. "He said your name was Macy. Do you have a last name?"

I bow my head. "Lowell." I look back up in time to see the widening of his eyes. Hum... has he heard of me? That would be surprising, considering Marvin tries to ensure I don't exist on record.

He schools his features back to his bored mask and holds out a hand, raising a brow. I look at Warren, and he nods as if telling me not to offend this influential man. I place my hand into Jax's, and it's as if a zap of electricity zips through my body.

Jax smirks as he kisses the top of my hand. "It's a pleasure to meet you, Miss Lowell." He pulls away and winks, then turns away, releasing my hand as he does. What the hell was that?

"Do you know him, Macy?" Warren whispers beside me.

I shake my head. "No. This is the first time I've met him."

Warren snorts. "It seems you have charmed one of the Steepe brothers. I would be careful if I were you."

Shaking myself out of the haze Jax seemed to put me in, I look up at Warren. "Why?"

He chuckles. "Those brothers share everything."

Brows knitting, I ask, "Share everything?"

He hands me a champagne flute. "They share everything." He wiggles his brows as if that helps. Then he rolls his eyes and whispers in my ear, "They all fuck the same woman."

I gasp. "What?!"

He pulls away, laughing. "They share women. I've heard it's to make sure a woman doesn't break them apart. I heard that the oldest brother had a girlfriend who the others didn't trust. The woman ended up betraying them, and that's how their oldest brother was killed."

"Their oldest brother?"

"I think his name was Grayson. He was originally in charge of the Underground until he was murdered."

Shooting back my entire flute of champagne, I place it on the tray of a passing busboy. "And why are you giving me this warning?"

He points toward the corner of the room. My eyes follow until they land on Silas. Warren steps closer as he whispers, "He's now in charge of everything, and word is, he's looking for his brother's killer. That man doesn't trust anyone. Only his brothers."

"I still don't understand why you are warning me," I whisper back.

"One brother has his eyes on you. But they aren't your typical rich men."

I stiffen. "What's that supposed to mean?"

He nips at my ear. "Word has spread about you, sweetheart. A cunt made of gold, but you steal from your wealthier clients. I've been told the pussy is worth it, though. But the Steepe brothers are a whole other breed."

I bite my lip. "And what type of breed is that?" I ask.

He snickers. "Wolves, sweetheart. Their last name is Steepe for a reason. They would kill you if you stole from them. My advice? Stick to our breed. We don't mind having money stolen from a creature like you."

I wrinkle my nose at his words. Creature. He makes me sound like a dog. He must see something in my face because he smiles and says, "A siren with beauty and sweet pussy is worth any price. We're rich. We can make back the money you steal easily."

Well, I will no longer feel bad about stealing from them, no matter how small the emotion was. These fuckers have been laughing as I stole from them. Well, then. I'll ensure I make out like a queen tonight. I snatch another glass of champagne from a passing waiter and hand it to Warren. I'll get him drunk as hell, strip him down, and make him think he had the best night of his life. Then, I'll steal everything I want.

I give him a sensual smile. "Drink up, Warren. We have a night full of fun and fucking ahead."

He smiles as he downs the glass, and I hand him another. He continues drinking glass after glass, and I laugh when I see his eyes slowly get glassy. His smile looks lop-sided as he slurs, "Let's have some fun!"

I nod as I help him out of the mansion and smile at the valet. "This is Mr. Carmichael. He's a bit drunk. If you could call for his driver, that would be great."

The young man nods and speaks into an earpiece. We stand there for a moment, waiting, then the male nods at us. "He should be here shortly."

"Thank you so much."

We don't have to wait long before the chauffeur pulls up. He jumps out and opens the rear door for us. I shove Warren in, and he laughs as he slides across the seat. I slide in next to him.

Warren smiles drunkenly up at me. "Tonight is going to be amazing, sweetheart. I'm going to rock your world."

I stifle a laugh as I say, "I'm sure you will." *Just not in the way you think.* After a few minutes, we pull to a stop in front of a high-rise apartment building in the area we consider downtown. The chauffeur opens the door, and I smile my thanks. I turn to help Warren out of the car, then look at the other guy. "Thanks for driving. I'll make sure he gets up to his place."

The driver nods. "He's the top level. The penthouse."

I nod, then make my way to the entrance, helping Warren walk. Damn, maybe I overdid it on the alcohol? I make my way through the revolving doors and smile at the doorman. He nods, recognizing Warren next to me. We make it to the elevators, and I press the button for the penthouse. The elevator takes us all the way to the top, and the doors open to another door down the hall.

"Do you have your keys, Warren?"

He nods enthusiastically and rifles through his pockets. He finally pulls out a pair of keys and holds them out to me. I take them, rolling my eyes. I try the fanciest key first, and it opens the door instantly. I turn to Warren. "Alright, you go to the bedroom, and I'll be there shortly. I'm going to find a bathroom and freshen up."

He smiles. "Okay! Don't take too long." He stumbles off in the direction I assume leads to his bedroom. I wait until he's out of sight to look around the house, taking measures of the items that I could steal. I give it a few minutes before following after him to the bedroom. I'm smiling before I ever make it to his door because I can hear the loud snoring coming from inside. I peek through the doorway to find he hasn't even undressed but is passed out cold, face first on his bed.

I giggle softly as I wander around the house. This is going to be my biggest haul yet!

CHAPTER FIVE
MACY

I laugh as I open the door to my apartment and throw my keys on the table by the door. I make my way into my small living room and plop down on the couch, smiling at the suitcase of shit I pillaged from Warren's house. The great thing about it being in a suitcase is the doorman didn't even stop me, and neither did the driver who drove me home.

Setting the suitcase down on the coffee table in front of me, I open it and squeal at my haul. I found a stash of jewelry and gifts that Warren kept in a closet. I assume he gave these to women he tried to pursue. I stole every single piece I could find. I also stole a few of his nice button-down shirts. What? Those shirts are silky smooth and are great as nightshirts.

My smile slides off my face, and my mood is immediately ruined when my phone squeals from my pocket. I have a specific ringtone set for Marvin, so I know who it is from the first bar and could choose to ignore it or answer. Decisions... decisions. I didn't end my call with him on good terms this morning, so I should probably answer. Sighing, I slide my thumb across the screen. "Did you get a great payday from my John this evening?" I was smart. I made Warren pay me before we went back to his place and he passed out. I make sure they pay me before I steal. I'm not that stupid.

"Yes, that's not why I'm calling."

Groaning, I ask, "So why are you calling then? I'm not fucking you, if that's why."

He growls and snaps, "I didn't fucking call for a booty call, Macy!"

"I had a long night, Marv. Get to the fucking point."

He snarls, "Why the fuck am I getting a call from one of the Steepe brothers?"

I recoil in surprise. "What?"

"I've had several calls from Jax Steepe tonight. Why would he know who you are, and why would he be calling me?"

"Um... I'm not sure. I met him briefly tonight at the event my John took me to. He introduced us, but I didn't think anything of it. What does he want?"

"He wants to hire you as an escort. Indefinitely. He's offered to pay a weekly sum for your services."

I snort. "And you're going to allow me to be an escort for Jax Steepe?"

"I'd let you be a fucking whore for any one of the Steepe brothers for what they are willing to pay."

Well, that gets my attention. "What are they paying?"

"They are willing to pay ten thousand a day for your services."

Ten thousand dollars a day! That's seventy thousand for a week, and they want me indefinitely? Well, I suppose there are worse guys to be an escort for. "So when do I start?"

"That's my girl! I'll call him and let him know you are enthusiastic about this opportunity. Don't fuck this up!"

"How the fuck would I?"

He growls over the phone. "Your attitude is less than pleasurable in male company. Put a fucking leash on it! Do your damn job, and get me my money. I don't even care if you steal from them."

I'm silent. How the hell did he know I was stealing from my Johns?

"Did you think I didn't know?" He laughs. "It's my job to know what you're doing, little doll. I'm in charge of your father's debt. If you step even a toe out of line, your father suffers. So. Make me proud with this job." He cackles as he hangs up.

I want to throw my phone across the room, but I control myself. It doesn't matter that he knows I steal. He doesn't know what I steal or even how much money I have saved up from the shit I've stolen. This job will be like all the others.

I'm startled awake the next morning by a knock on my door. I grumble as I make sure I'm at least wearing something. I smile at the silk button-down shirt. I'm so glad I stole this shirt. I look through the peephole before opening the door. With a yawn, I say, "Morning, Rem. What's up?"

He looks me up and down before his brows knit together. "There are three males in the lobby who say they are here to pick you up."

I squint, wondering who he could possibly be talking about before my eyes widen. "Shit! Um... okay. Yeah, just go back down and allow them up."

His brows knit even more as he says, "Are you alright, Macy?"

I smile up at him. "Just fine, Rem. It's another job. But, I'll probably be gone for a little bit. So, don't worry that something may have happened to me."

He stares at me for another moment before nodding. "As you wish, Miss Macy."

I watch as he walks back to the elevator, then I close the door and look around my apartment. Fuck! What the fuck am I going to take with me? I have absolutely no normal clothes whatsoever. The more I think about it, the more I realize I don't actually have a life outside of work.

Huffing out a sigh, I move to my bedroom to grab a suitcase for my shoes. I know I at least need to take those. Should I pack a few sexy outfits as well? Before I can think too much about it, there's another knock on my door. I look down at myself and realize I haven't put on a pair of pants.

Shrugging, I make my way to the door, swinging it open to find three very large figures. My mouth drops open as I look between them. Jax is standing in front, while the other two are standing slightly behind him. I shut my mouth, rubbing the back of my head. "Um... I didn't realize you guys were coming to pick me up or I would have been ready."

Jax waves his hand in the air and says, "It's not a problem, we can wait."

I look behind me and then back out at them. "If you want to come in you can. I don't have much to pack."

Jax nods as he makes his way past me into the apartment. Silas nods as he passes me. Luka is the last one through the door, and he gives me a small smile, which puts his dimples on display. He points down at my bare legs. "You may want to put some pants on, it's a bit chilly out."

I snort out a laugh, then cover my mouth, remembering that I need to NOT be myself around these guys.

Luka smiles as he walks past me. "You don't have to pretend with us. We don't care."

I arch a brow in question. "What's that supposed to mean?"

Jax speaks up. "You're a wolf—like us. Like calls to like, darling. Although, I feel your wolf hasn't emerged. Maybe you're still a cub."

Closing the door, I spin to face Jax. "A wolf like you? And that means?"

Silas sighs and says, "We know what Marvin does to his females. Although, I was curious when Jax mentioned you. You aren't on the books as one the women he has as a professional escort or prostitute."

I arch a brow, not sure if I'm supposed to say anything to confirm or deny why I'm not on the books.

Silas finds a spot on the couch in my living room, then puts his ankle on his knee as he pierces me with his hazel eyes. "Why would he have a woman who makes more in one night than several of his other escorts do in a week, not on the books?"

I remain silent for a moment before saying, "If I knew the answer to that question, what makes you think I'd tell you?"

He shrugs. "I don't expect you to answer at all. I'm planning on figuring it out for myself. You don't trust us, and to be quite honest, I don't trust you. But, I tend to indulge my brother's curiosities." His eyes narrow on me before he continues, "Though, don't take my indulgence for my brother's curiosity as a weakness. I will kill you if you try to betray us."

My eyes widen, and I hear Jax hiss, "Silas!"

Silas's eyes don't waver from mine. He stares at me as I think about his words. I understand, though. He wants to protect his brothers from what happened to his oldest sibling. I nod. "Understood."

He nods as he says, "Now that that's said, do you any need help packing?"

I shake my head and reply, "I don't have much. Just a suitcase of shoes and a few dressy clothes."

His brows pinch for a moment before he nods. "That will be fixed. Luka, can you grab her suitcase and take it to the car?"

Luka nods, turning to me. "Which way?"

Completely confused as to what is going on, I point toward my bedroom. He smiles and passes by me to get my suitcase.

Jax clears his throat. I turn in his direction to find him pointing at my legs. I look down to see that I still haven't put pants on. "You should probably get some pants on."

"Right..." I make my way to my bedroom to find Luka trying to close the suitcase full of shoes. I can't stop the giggle that slips through.

He looks over his shoulder at me and then back down at the suitcase. "Are you sure all these shoes are necessary?"

I smirk and walk over to him. "You push down and I'll zip." He nods as he puts his weight down on the suitcase. I manage to get it shut on the third try. "And to answer your question, yes that many shoes are necessary."

He huffs out a breath as he drops the bag on the floor. "This could be considered a deadly weapon. I'm just saying, if you managed to drop this out a window you could easily kill someone."

I laugh as I shuffle my way over to my closet and pull out a pair of yoga pants. I put them on and slip into a pair of fuzzy slippers, turning to find Luka is still there. I arch a brow in question, and he seems to shake himself out of whatever daze he was lost in. A blush creeps across his cheeks, and I grin as I ask, "What?"

He shakes his head and moves toward my door. I laugh as I race in front of him to stop him from leaving. "What?"

He huffs out a sigh before looking at me. "Your laugh is pretty."

My eyes widen at his words. "My... my laugh?"

I watch as his blush deepens across his cheeks, and he nods. "Yeah. Your smile is beautiful too. You should do it more." He takes off past me as I stand there dumbfounded.

My laugh? My smile? I don't think I've ever been complimented on anything other than my looks or my vagina, to be honest. I feel my cheeks heat. I haven't laughed for real in a long time. All my laughs these days are about as fake as my smiles.

I hear my name called down the hall, and I jump. "Coming!" Maybe this job won't be as bad as I thought.

CHAPTER SIX

MACY

My mouth gapes open when we pull to a stop in front of an eight-story building. I'm slightly confused because it looks like one of those old manufacturing buildings, but it also has a huge sign out front that reads: Tartarus. The most popular nightclub in the city. I point at the building and ask, "Is there a reason we are going to a club?"

The youngest brother, Luka, smiles at me before explaining, "We own the building." He points up at the upper levels. "The top four floors are our personal living spaces."

"Still wondering why you live above a nightclub."

"I used to run the club until a friend took it over for me. We still own it; I just no longer show my face as the manager," Luka says as he steps out of the car and holds out a hand for me to take. "Ready to see your new home?"

New home? I haven't had a home in years. Even my apartment isn't really my home; it's just somewhere I live. "Home?" I ask, arching a brow.

He shrugs as Jax comes around to meet us. He gives me a boyish smirk as he says, "For as long as you want."

For as long as I want? Aren't they paying for me to stay with them? Wouldn't that make it for as long as they want, not me? Also, what is up with these men, and why are they giving me butterflies? I've never had butterflies before. I've only been with these guys for a few hours, and I'm already trying not to blush as my stomach flutters. Trying to get a grip on myself, I take Luka's outstretched hand and say, "Don't you mean for as long as you want me here?"

I jump slightly when Silas's voice surprises me. "My brother doesn't often say something he doesn't mean. If he says you are welcome here until you see otherwise, that is what he means."

The deep timber of his voice makes his words seem harsh, but I feel like that may just be his attitude in general. I watch as he leads the way to a side door off of the main nightclub entrance. Luka ushers me along with him as Jax takes up the rear.

We enter an elevator, and I turn in time to see Silas push the button for the fifth floor. I feel awkward standing in an elevator with these powerful men. Do they not realize how much power they exude without even meaning to? The elevator doors open into a wide open concept apartment. Silas leads the way.

He gestures around and says, "This is the main living area. There's a kitchen fully equipped with everything you could imagine. If you want to watch TV or anything, we have every streaming service you could possibly want. If there's something you can't find, let me know." He turns toward the left corner. "There are steps that lead up to the other levels if you don't want to use the elevator. The bedrooms are on the sixth and seventh floors. And the top level is where our offices are."

Turning to face me, he points below him and says, "The fourth floor is the gym. The third is the office for the nightclub. The second and first levels are strictly for the club. If you would like to visit the nightclub, just let one of us know so we can let Roy know that you will be down there and that you are with us."

I stand there looking between the brothers, mouth agape. Jax smirks as he asks, "You good?"

Shaking myself, I nod. "Yes. Just a bit overwhelmed."

Silas nods, stone-faced. Does he ever smile, or does he always look that serious? "Do you have any questions?" he asks.

My palms grow sweaty, and I pull my hand out of Luka's. Wiping them on my pants, I take a deep breath. Why the fuck am I so nervous to ask this question? I work as an escort, just ask the fucking question, Macy! "Um... is there something I need to do for you guys?"

Luka looks completely confused by the question. Jax looks between his brothers before looking back at me and raising a brow. "Do you mean to ask if you need to pay us with sex?" I watch as Jax looks back over to Silas. Looking at Silas, I almost miss it, but I see the twitch of his eyebrow as his eyes darken. He looks pissed.

Silas's hands curl into fists before relaxing. He shakes his head. "You do not owe us anything to live here."

I snort a laugh and say, "Nothing in this world is free. What do you want from me? You're not paying Marvin that type of money without wanting something in return."

Silas relaxes his stance a bit before shrugging. "My brother wanted your company."

"And my company is worth that type of money without sex?"

Silas shrugs again as he makes his way towards the stairs. "Believe it or not, not every male wants sex from a woman." He disappears upstairs before I can say anything back.

Luka comes up beside me and bumps my shoulder. "We don't have a room set up for you yet, but you can use the guest room. We will figure out the clothes situation while you get settled."

Jax gestures me toward the stairs. "The guest room is on the floor right above us. You'll have it to yourself, since ours are on the seventh floor. We'll let you get settled. If you need anything, we'll be on the top floor for a bit."

I huff out a sigh but nod as I follow behind them up the stairs. We part ways, and they continue up to the top floor. I make my way toward the only closed door because when I peek into the other rooms, I find them completely empty. I open the door with a flourish as I pull my lonely suitcase behind me. I have to stop myself from stumbling as I walk through the door though, because, HOLY SHIT! I look around the room completely amazed. This is the guest room? It looks like a five-star resort in here.

I can't stop the small smile that creases my face as I let my suitcase fall, and I run across the room to jump on the bed. Oh... god... yes. I make a snow angel in the down comforter that makes me feel like I'm floating on a cloud. I think I'm going to like this.

Silas

I huff out a breath as I take a seat at my desk. Why the hell did Jax want to bring that woman into our home? Women are all the same. All they want is to get with the most powerful man to help further their own status. Then, when a more powerful man comes along, they betray you and leave you for dead. I grind my teeth as I think about my dead brother. I hope that woman got what was coming to her because if I ever see her conniving bitch face again, I will kill her myself.

I sigh again as I rest my head on my palm. All women aren't the same though. There has only ever been one woman I've allowed to sink her fingers into my heart. As if thinking of her somehow summoned her, my phone begins to ring. My brothers walk through the doorway as I look down at the screen.

I can't stop the smirk that tugs at my lips when I answer, "Hey, darling."

"Don't you dare darling me, Silas! I know what you did!"

I snicker as I lean back in my chair. "What do you mean, Jane?" My brothers start chuckling as they take a seat on the open chairs in front of my desk.

"We just got back from our honeymoon, and my shower has completely changed. The guys swear up and down that it wasn't them. So that leaves you."

I try to reply in my most innocent tone, but I'm pretty sure it doesn't fool her. "Why am I to blame? It could have been Jax or Luka."

She snorts out a laugh. "Oh, I know it was all of you, but you were the mastermind."

I roll my eyes as I concede. "Fine. But, don't tell me you don't love it because I know for damn sure that you do."

"I do love it, but it's too much!" she screeches.

"It wasn't too much. It's our wedding present to you. I'm not ripping it all out because that would be even more work, so you better just accept it now and say thank you."

I hear her huff out a breath before she's silent for a moment. I'm about to ask if she's okay when she finally whispers, "Thank you."

I can hear the emotion in her voice. I look at my brothers and they each arch a brow in worry. Rubbing the back of my neck, completely uncomfortable dealing with emotions, I say, "You're welcome, Jane."

She sighs. "Well, I meant to chew you out for the gift, but I guess I'll just enjoy it if I must."

I smirk as I say, "I hope you do. Now, I'm sure your men are wanting your attention."

She laughs and says, "You're right. They are all watching me and waiting for me to hang up."

I chuckle. "I'll talk to you later."

"Bye, Si. Love you!"

I grunt in reply. "Yeah. You too." She laughs as she hangs up. I look down at my phone with a smirk before looking back up at my brothers.

Jax is smirking as he asks, "Was she trying to yell at us for installing that new shower?"

I nod. "Yeah."

"I hope it helps her," Luka says with a wistful smile.

"Me too." I really do hope it helps. After she had been abducted and tortured, she hadn't been able to take a shower for months. Someone had to be in the shower with her or she would have a panic attack. The horrors of almost being drowned becoming too much. The guys told us that she had finally been able to get in the shower by herself, but she couldn't wash her hair if she didn't have control over the water.

So while they were gone, we installed a completely new shower system. She now has six jets on the wall that will hit her from her knees up to her mid-back. Then there is a removable shower head that when on, will hit her mid-back. None of the water will hit her face unless she wants it to. She will have complete control, which is what she needs. She can also change the shower head to a different setting, so the water doesn't spray or pour on her face. That should help with her PTSD and flashbacks.

Even if I haven't told her I love her, she knows. She knows how I feel about saying the words, and she's never pushed me. I remember asking her once, "Why don't you care if I say the words back?"

She only smiled up at me and replied, "I don't need the words from you, Si."

With a frown, I asked, "You don't need the words?"

She just shrugged. "I mean, I love hearing them. Jax and Luka say it all the time, but that's just how they are. With you... you don't have to say it. I can see it. I can feel it."

My eyes widened. "How?"

She smiled as she explained, "You show me. You remember the oddest things and show that you love me through your actions. You can tell when I need a hug or when I need someone to talk to. You can tell when I'm upset or stressed. You buy me my favorite candy to cheer me up or go out and buy coffee when I forget."

I arched a brow, unconvinced. "The guys do that for you all the time."

She snorted out a laugh. "They do, and I love it. They are the men I love, and they will do anything to make me happy. But, you're the older brother I never got. It means something different when it comes from you."

I hadn't really understood love until that day. Love is when the other person understands and accepts you for who you are. All of your bumps and bruises. Tears and scrapes. Broken and shattered pieces. Love doesn't always have to be romantic. She loves and accepts me for who I am. And I love her all the more for it. I may not say I love her with words, but I for damn sure make sure that I show her every chance I get.

CHAPTER SEVEN
MACY

I'm startled out of my thoughts by a knock at the door. I look around, realizing I've been snuggling in bed for hours. "Come in."

I lift my head to see the door slowly open and Luka poke his head through. He greets me with a soft smile, which makes those adorable dimples of his show. Now that I think about it, he seems to be the quiet one. Nothing like the guy I saw at the party. I assumed he would be the playboy, but maybe that was just a mask.

"Hey, sorry to disturb you, but I wanted to let you know that dinner is ready."

I groan as I roll off the bed. "You're lucky I love food more than I love this bed."

He smirks as he opens the door wide enough for me to walk through. "Good to know I can bribe you with food. I'm assuming the room is to your liking?"

I arch a brow at him, debating if he's serious or not. Gauging by the growing furrow in his brow the longer I'm silent, I think he's serious. "Of course, I like the room."

He nods with a smile. "Good. If you didn't, we could have moved you to one you liked more."

Shaking my head, I say, "The room is fine. I just wish I had clothes other than what I brought with me."

He nods as we make our way toward the elevator. "Clothes have been ordered and should be here tomorrow."

I'm not sure if I should be happy that I don't have to go out and buy my own clothes or upset that they bought me clothes without my input. "You guys bought me clothes?"

He shrugs. "We picked out an assortment. More for casual wear than anything else. But we had a personal shopper pick out your intimates." He chuckles as he presses the elevator button. "I wouldn't be surprised if Jax picked out a few dresses, though."

Now that I think about it, Jax does seem more the ladies' man type out of the two of them. At the party where we met, Jax was the one who ignored me at first and walked past, but he was the one who introduced himself first too. He's also the one who requested I come and stay here.

"He seems like the kind of man who can get anyone he wants in his bed, so why request me?" I am talking more to myself than anything, but I must have spoken loud enough for Luka to hear because he responds.

"My brother only plays the ladies' man. He hasn't dated much or slept with anyone for quite some time."

My eyes widen at his words as we step into the elevator. I can't stop myself from asking, "Why doesn't he date anymore?"

Luka doesn't answer as he leads me out of the elevator and into the living space. We make our way over to the kitchen, and he walks around the large island toward the cooking area. Pointing over his shoulder toward the chairs at the island, he says, "Sit."

Shrugging, I do as I'm told and watch as he pulls down a few plates. He fills one plate with food, then turns and slides it to me. I look down to find fried chicken, mashed potatoes and gravy, as well as sweet-glazed carrots. I take a deep breath in and almost let out an embarrassing moan. Damn, that smells amazing! I haven't had a home-cooked meal in years; I honestly couldn't tell you the last time. I look back up with a smirk as I tease, "This looks delicious, but it doesn't get you out of answering my question."

He grins as he plates himself a heaping pile of food before coming around and sitting next to me. I begin dipping bits of fried chicken into my mashed potatoes and gravy. He looks down at his food for a moment before turning to me. "It's not really my place to tell you why my brother doesn't date or have flings with women anymore. But... I guess I can tell you that he finally saw what true love looked like. He wants that. He wants to find a woman who will love him for him rather than the money or status he can provide her." He looks back down at his food and pushes his potatoes around for a moment before admitting in a hushed voice, "We are all looking for that, I guess."

I pause my chewing as I look at him. He has this wistful look on his face, as if he's thinking about someone in particular. I feel a twinge of emotion pulse in my chest, but I'm not sure what it is, which sort of annoys me. I've never felt this emotion before. Ignoring it, I swallow my bite and give him a shrug. "That makes sense, I guess. I wouldn't know, though." I look over to find him watching me. I give him a smile, but I don't think it reaches my eyes. "You can't miss something you've never had."

He frowns and says, "I don't think it's missing something we've never had. More like we yearn for something someone else has found."

I open my mouth to reply when we hear a ruckus behind us. I look over my shoulder to find Jax shoving Silas as he runs past. "I get to eat first!" Jax yells as he heads our direction.

Silas growls behind him and calls after him, "It's not a fucking race! Just because you lost the bet, doesn't mean that you suddenly can win at something else."

Jax snickers as he begins piling his plate high with food. "It does if I say it does. Therefore, I'm the winner."

Silas walks into the kitchen at a casual pace. "You can say whatever you want, brother. Doesn't make it so." As soon as Jax is done, Silas begins serving himself. Jax comes around the counter and sits on my free side with a grin.

"How are you liking it here so far?"

I shrug. "I've only been here for a few hours so the jury is still out." I shove another bite of food in my mouth to avoid the next question I can see on his lips.

"So was I right?" Luka questions beside me.

Jax groans, and I can see the smirk on Silas's face as he comes around the island to sit beside Luka. "You both were wrong. I won the bet."

Luka arches a brow. "Really? Hum, didn't see that one coming."

I'm trying really hard not to ask what the hell they are talking about, but my curiosity wins out. "What bet?"

Silas's smirk vanishes as he narrows his eyes at me. Was I not supposed to ask? I'm about to say nevermind when Jax answers, "We had a bet going about our friend's reaction to something we did. Surprisingly, Silas won."

I turn toward Jax as I ask, "What did he win?"

"The satisfaction of knowing I won," Silas responds before he begins eating.

I arch a brow, looking in his direction. "Well, that seems boring."

He shrugs. "I like winning."

Well, you can't argue with that, can you? Although, I'm still extremely curious about how he won the bet. He seems so distant from everyone and everything. But I have seen small instances where he's nice and seems to have normal feelings. I guess I'll find out more about these brothers considering I'll be living here for an unknown length of time.

CHAPTER EIGHT
MACY

I've been here for a week, and so far, I have to admit, this is the best job I've had in years. My clothes came the day after I arrived, and Luka had been right. They had ordered a little bit of everything from band tees and jeans to business casual attire. There were also a few beautiful dresses, which I assume were picked by Jax.

I've also learned several things about the guys this past week. Luka is definitely the nice, quiet one. He always asks if I'm doing alright and if there is anything I need. I have mentioned several of my favorite snacks, and by the next day, they are in the pantry. Although, I have mentioned it when the others were around, so it could be any of them, but my guess is Luka.

Jax smokes. A lot. Well, maybe I shouldn't say a lot. I've noticed he smokes when he is really stressed out or aggravated. Which seems to be more often than not. I would say something, but it's not really my place. Right? But he is nice and sweet, so maybe I should say something? He loves to tease me, and sometimes I feel like he's flirting with me. Which I have no idea how to handle. I've never had a guy flirt with me who didn't want something in return.

Then there's Silas. He seems extremely protective of his brothers, which I can respect. He takes his job as the head of the family seriously. But I feel like he's always too serious. I've never seen him smile; I've only caught glimpses of him smirking at something Jax or Luka says before it disappears. I wish I could see that side of him more. He also doesn't seem to trust anyone except his brothers, which I suppose includes me. The not trusting part. Though, I don't trust them either, so I guess that's fair.

I take a sip of my coffee and let out a sigh. I still haven't figured out why I'm here, either. No one has made a move to request sex or even show me off. I'm not really sure what to think about it, honestly. The elevator dings from behind me, pulling me out of my thoughts, and I look over my shoulder to see Jax exit in nothing but a pair of basketball shorts. Low-slung basketball shorts.

Ladies, you know that beautiful V we all love? The one that leads directly to the naughty bits? Yep. That V. Well, this man has it, and I have to force my mouth to stay closed so I'm not gaping like a fish. Because, holy shit, this man is fine. His hair is up in a messy bun, but a few strands have escaped and are stuck to the sides of his sweaty face. His toned body is on full display as he makes his way over toward me. He still has perspiration gleaming across his tanned chest. Man... I wonder what he tastes like? I could just lick him and... wait... WAIT! What the hell am I thinking? I do NOT want to lick this man! Okay, well, maybe that is a lie, but that's between us girls, right? Girl pack!

My eyes meet his, and I realize he's smirking. Refusing to blush, I clear my throat and ask, "Did you have a good workout?"

His smirk grows into a smile as he nods. "I did. Did you have a good night's rest?" He walks over to the cabinets and pulls out a shaker cup.

"I did. Thank you for asking." I watch as he puts in a few scoops of several different powders before filling it with water. He shakes the cup a few times, then takes a large gulp. I point to the cup. "What's in that?"

He looks at the cup before looking back up at me. "Vitamins and a few other things to help my body recover from a workout."

I nod. That makes sense, I guess. We are quiet for a moment before he speaks up again. "We have an event tonight that we need to make an appearance at. Do you want to come along?"

I arch a brow as I ask, "I have the option?"

He shrugs. "If you want to come you can, if not, then don't. We aren't going to make you."

My brows furrow in confusion. I've never had the option of not going before. "Wasn't that the point of you buying my time? To flaunt me in front of the cameras and show me off to the world?"

His eyes widen for a moment as if surprised I would even think that. His surprise shifts into amusement as he smirks and says, "If I wanted to flaunt a woman at parties, I wouldn't have to pay her to do so."

My cheeks heat at his words, and I'm not sure if it's from embarrassment or anger. "So, why pay for me then?"

He comes around the island to lean against the side next to me. Smiling down at me, he says, "Well, I wouldn't have the pleasure of your company otherwise. Would I?"

My eyes narrow. "And why would you want the pleasure of my company, Jax?"

He arches a brow as he pushes off the counter. "I thought you would have realized that by now, Mace."

Mace? When did we start having nicknames for each other? "Realize what?"

He bends down so our faces are only inches apart and smirks when I gasp at how close he is. His eyes roam over my face before spearing me with his gaze. "You're a wolf, just like us." He shrugs as he continues, "A cub right now, but a wolf nonetheless."

"What does that even mean?" I breathe out.

He smiles as he pulls away. "It means that you are meant to be one of us."

My mouth drops at his words. What's that supposed to mean? I'm supposed to be one of them? Does he mean that he wants me to become part of his world? But ... he made it sound like I was supposed to be with all of them.

He just smiles as he walks away. I'm still shocked and silent as he shouts over his shoulder, "I do hope you accompany us tonight, little wolf. We could have so much fun."

CHAPTER NINE
MACY

Needless to say, I am now standing in front of my mirror in my lingerie, trying to pick out a dress to wear tonight. I've never had a problem picking out an outfit before, but I am now. Which seems to irritate me more than anything else. Why do I care what I look like? This shouldn't matter, but somewhere deep down, I find that I want to look beautiful instead of sexy. I've looked sexy and fuckable most of my life. I want something different.

There's a knock at the door, and before I realize that I'm in nothing but my bra and underwear, I say, "Come in." I walk out of the closet and around the corner of my bathroom door to see Silas slip inside. Silas? I look down at myself, then back up to see his eyes meet mine. His eyes don't leave my own which is surprising considering what I'm wearing or lack thereof. Most men would take the opportunity to feast their eyes on my body.

"I see you're not ready yet." His voice isn't cold like usual but still matter of fact.

I arch a brow. Unable to help myself, I ask, "What gave it away?"

I see the slight tilt of his lips before he can hide it. "It's hard to miss that you are in nothing other than your undergarments."

I can't stop the smirk that crosses my lips. "You looked?"

He huffs out a sigh and says, "It's hard to miss, Macy. I am trying to be a gentleman by not looking, but you are making it hard by continuing this conversation."

I huff out a sigh as I turn back into my closet. "I'm having a hard time picking out what to wear. Jax didn't mention what type of event this is."

"I find it hard to believe that the type of event has ever stopped you from picking out something to wear," he says, standing outside my bathroom, making sure not to enter.

I bite my lower lip, debating whether or not to give Silas a truth I'm not entirely proud of confessing. I must have stayed quiet for too long as his voice rings out in the silence. "Macy?"

I release a self-deprecating growl as I admit, "I've always looked sexy and fuckable. I want to look different for once. Which is proving to be an issue of picking out an outfit."

He's silent for a moment before he asks, "Would you like me to pick it out?"

I debate his words for a moment before sighing. "If you wouldn't mind?"

He enters the closet, not letting his eyes roam over me as he takes a look around, evaluating his options. I did bring a few dresses from my collection, but I don't think they would work for this evening. I watch as he ignores the dresses I've brought in favor of the new ones that came with the delivery. I haven't had a chance to look through all of them yet, but I'm sure they are all beautiful.

I watch as he shifts through some of them before nodding at one . He pulls it out, giving it a critical eye, before turning to me. "I think this will work for tonight. What do you think?"

What do I think? I think it's beautiful in a very classic way. It's an off-the-shoulder black dress with a wide black belt that would cinch around my waist, giving me an amazing figure. It would hug my curves, giving me an hourglass look that cuts off right below my knees, so it's short but not too short. I nod with a smile. "It's beautiful."

He hands me the dress, then turns back around to look through my heels. I was pleasantly surprised to find that shoes had also been delivered. I slip into the dress, turning toward the mirror. My eyes widen at the woman I see in the reflection. She's mesmerizing. I'm startled out of my thoughts by Silas's voice.

"These will look good with the dress. A pop of color, but they won't take away from the classic look you want."

I take the shoebox from him to find a pair of simple red pumps with a two inch heel. "Thank you," I say as I slip them on.

He shrugs. "You're welcome." He points toward my hair as he says, "You could put half your hair up in a loose bun. Your natural, loose curls look good with the dress."

My face heats as I look into the mirror and arrange my hair as he suggests. Once I'm done, I'm in awe of the woman I see staring back at me. I no longer look like a fuckable escort, rather, an elegant woman. It is odd seeing her. I feel myself flush more when I notice Silas looking at me in the mirror. There's a softness in his eyes that I haven't seen before. He can't be thinking about me with that look, can he? I can't stop myself from asking, "How do you know so much about all this?"

He shakes himself out of whatever thoughts he was lost in before his eyes meet mine. I see his walls come back up, but surprisingly, the softness is still there as he says, "I've had to help my sister out with clothing options."

I arch a brow. As far as I knew, the brothers didn't have a sister. "Sister?" I can't help but ask.

He shrugs and answers, "A chosen sister. She sort of adopted us without asking."

Before I can ask anything else, a voice interrupts, "Mace! Are you ready to go yet?"

I snort out a laugh and say, "In the bathroom, Jax."

"Does that mean I can come in?"

"Yes, Jax. You can come in." I smile as I turn toward the door. He comes around the corner and freezes, his mouth dropping open as he takes me in. I feel my face flush under his gaze. I look down at myself and then back up at him. "Do I look okay?" I ask in a whisper.

His mouth snaps closed as his eyes meet mine. He nods and says, "Of course. You look beautiful, Mace."

My smile grows. "Thank you."

He smiles back, and for once, I feel like it's a genuine smile. Not forced or playful, but a real smile. He offers me his elbow and asks, "Would you mind if I escorted you to the elevator?"

I can't stop the giggle that erupts as I nod. I lay my hand in the crook of his elbow as he leads me out of my room and into the elevator. Silas walks quietly behind us. I briefly catch the look on his face before he turns to face the door of the elevator as it closes. His brows were pinched in thought as he frowned.

I shake the thought away as the doors slide open. Silas exits first, and that's when I see Luka. He's dressed up a bit more than his usual attire for events. He's still wearing jeans, but they are a dark wash, with a black button-down shirt, untucked. His normally messy, wispy hair is now slicked back. He looks good.

He smiles at me, and I give him a shy wave as I say, "Hey, Luka. You look nice."

His smile grows to show off those amazing dimples as he says, "Nothing compares to you, Macy. You look gorgeous."

I duck my head, trying to hide my blush. "Thank you." I haven't thanked a man so much in my life for compliments, and I'm now thanking three in a single day.

Jax gives my hand a squeeze as we continue toward the garage. "We have the most magnificent woman on our arms tonight, brothers."

Luka comes to walk beside me as he says, "You'll get no argument from me, brother."

For the first time in my life, I'm speechless. I'm not sure what to do with all of the compliments. I've never felt beautiful. I've always felt like an object for men to show off. I may be expensive, but I've always felt cheap. Tonight though, I feel beautiful. I feel like I'm worth more than the money I charge for my time. I feel worth more than the object men covet. And that... is an amazing feeling.

CHAPTER TEN
MACY

I'm blinded by the photographer's flash as we exit the car. Surprisingly, Luka is the one who escorts me into the building, but what's even more shocking is that Silas and Jax waited for us to get out of the car before walking toward the building. Jax came to stand next to me, as Silas took the lead. Reporters screamed questions about me and what my relationship was to the guys, but they ignored everyone.

The doormen hold open the double-door entry, and I gasp in awe of the room as we walk inside. Sheer sheets of fabric are beautifully draped, decorating the ceiling with fairy lights strung up everywhere. I can't stop myself from whispering, "What is this event for again?"

Luka lowers his head enough to whisper back. "It's to promote the club we are opening in the next few months."

"What's the theme of the club?" I ask in curiosity.

Jax answers, "It's a club dedicated to Persephone."

My eyes widen. "As in the Queen of the Underworld?"

Jax nods as he says, "One and the same. The Underworld owns the Underground. Hades wanted a club dedicated to his wife. It's a bit tamer, and it will feature things that could only be found in fantasy."

I arch a brow. "Such as?"

He looks down at me with a smirk but answers, "Persephone is not only the Queen of the Underworld but the Goddess of Spring. It's a glimpse into that world of fantasy and the creatures that exist within."

I look around the room still in awe. Flowers decorate every surface. "What sort of creatures exist within that world?"

Luka is the one that answers this time. "Sirens, Arae, Basilisks, Daemons, and Nymphs are only a few."

"And how do you find these creatures?" I ask in curiosity.

Luka shrugs. "We pay people to play the part."

I nod. I can't argue with that. There are plenty of people out there who will gladly play a mythical creature to escape reality. We stop abruptly, and I try to look around Silas's opposing figure to see what stopped us. I groan when I see it's Warren. Well... fuck.

"Good evening, Warren. I do hope you are having a good time." Silas's voice comes across as polite, but there's a chill behind the words. Maybe I'm the only one who picks up on it because Warren greets him with a smile.

"This evening's festivities are favorable as always." Warren peers around Silas to greet the others, but his eyes widen when he sees me. I can tell he's surprised to find me with the brothers. He quickly covers his shock with a pleasant smile as he nods toward each brother in greeting. "Good evening, Jax and Luka."

His eyes turn cold when they meet mine. His polite smile turns to a sneer as he says, "Evening, Macy. Seems you've upgraded your status since our last meeting. Do they fuck you well enough?"

I'm about to give a snarky comeback, but it's interrupted by a growl. I jump a bit when the sound comes from beside me. I look up to find Jax glaring down at the man. "Watch how you speak to Miss Lowell, or you may find your money is not worth much at our casinos."

My eyes widen more when I watch Warren wince as Silas slams a hand down on his shoulder. His voice is dark and full of violence as he says, "Whether we fuck her or not is none of your concern. I also expect respect the next time you greet us. We are not friends, so do not greet us so informally." Silas pushes him away, and Warren stumbles as we walk by.

"Thank you," I say quietly as we walk away from Warren. "I didn't need you to protect me, though. I'm used to men thinking I'm a whore. I have thick skin."

Jax bumps my shoulder with his as he says, "We know. But you deserve someone to fight for you, even when you can fight for yourself."

I bite my lip, trying not to let his words affect me more than they already have. I don't know how to handle these men at all.

Silas adds from the front, "You are under our care, and we protect what is ours."

Ours? I look between Jax and Luka to find them looking down at me with a smile. Luka nods as he says, "He's right. But, enough about that overgrown asshat. Let's have some fun!"

I laugh as he pulls me away from the others and toward the dance floor. Jax cuts in a few times, and I'm pretty sure I'm dancing with both of them for several songs as well, while Silas watches from a distance. When I catch a few glimpses of him, he's watching us with a thoughtful look.

Silas

I watch as my brothers laugh and dance with Macy. She's a complete enigma to me. The more I'm around her, the more I want to learn, but I need to keep my distance. I'm the oldest now, and it's my job to keep my brothers safe. I can't let what happened to Grayson happen to my brothers or to myself. I won't let a woman into our circle again.

Though as I watch her laugh and smile, I can't help but think she's different. She handled herself nicely with that Warren fellow. I feel myself grimace at the thought of him. Fucking sleezeball. She looks so beautiful tonight, and to watch the spark in her eyes dim at his words... I couldn't stop myself from coming to her defense. Who is he to talk to her like that? I guarantee he's had his dipstick shoved in more holes than I can count. He has no room to judge her.

The corner of my lip tilts into a smile as I watch Jax dance horribly in a circle around Macy as she laughs. Luka isn't dancing much better, which makes the situation even more entertaining. I haven't seen my brothers laugh or smile as much as they have in the last week she has been with us.

Which causes me more worry rather than less. They are getting attached to her. That will be a problem when she leaves. It's inevitable. They always do one way or another. I need to remind them that she is only temporary, and we will eventually part ways.

My eyes drift down to the dress she's wearing. She looks beautiful in the one I picked out. I was surprised to find her in the closet looking completely lost. I couldn't stop myself from helping when she gave me that deer-in-the-headlights look. She had no idea what to wear. Sexy and fuckable had been her words. She didn't want to look sexy and fuckable.

What she didn't know was she always looked sexy and fuckable. But, I suppose my definition of sexy and fuckable differed greatly from hers. I huff out a sigh as I watch my brothers and the woman who crashed into our lives. If I am being completely honest, I don't regret letting Jax bring her to live with us.

Macy

I'm giggling as we walk out of the elevator. Luka is laughing as well, while Jax is still telling us a story of a time he had gone to an event and got completely plastered. He told us that he ended up standing on top of one of the tables, announcing that he was the king of sexy dancing, then proceeded to dance. Horribly. Luka and I both have tears streaming down our faces from laughing so hard.

Jax chuckles as he says, "It's really not that funny guys."

Luka snorts as he continues to laugh. "It's even funnier hearing it again."

Jax rolls his eyes but smiles. "Whatever. I'm heading to bed. See ya in the morning."

We wave at him as he makes his way over to the stairs. Silas clears his throat and says, "I'm going to head up to the office and do a few things before bed. If you need anything, just call or come on up." With a stiff nod, he follows after his brother.

My laughs die down as I realize that it's just Luka and I left. I watch as his smile turns shy, then he rubs the back of his neck. "I... um wanted to ask if you would mind coming up to my room? I want to show you something."

I stiffen a bit at his words. Tonight has been perfect, but I should have expected this. It's been an entire week. None of them have asked me to their rooms or asked for sex. My smile turns fake as I nod. "Yeah, of course." My stomach seems to sour as we make our way to the elevator.

It's silent the whole way up, but I notice Luka fiddling with his hands a lot as if he's nervous. Why would he be nervous? The elevator dings, and the doors open. I look around curiously since this is the guys' floor. Luka turns, opening the first door on the right.

I follow him in as he flicks the light on. He turns quickly with a nervous smile, holding out his hands. "Stay right there."

Now I'm confused. Sex usually starts on the bed but okay. I nod, which must be enough for him because he turns, running off toward his bathroom. It's only a few moments before he's jogging back out with a bag in hand.

He stops in front of me, holding it out as he rubs the back of his neck. He blows out a nervous breath, then says, "So I saw this at the mall the other day and thought of you. It's probably completely cheesy but…" He shrugs. "…I hope you like it."

I take the bag with furrowed brows. I slowly open it, expecting to find something sexual like usual, but my eyes widen at what I see. Inside the bag is a noodle Squishmallow. I look back up to Luka, not understanding. He's not looking at me, though, so I whisper, "Luka?"

His face is bright red as he looks down at the bag. "It's a noodle. Like Macaroni. Your name is Macy, and I noticed Jax calls you Mace. I thought Mac would be a good nickname, so when I saw the noodle, I couldn't pass up buying it for you." He lets out a nervous laugh as he continues, "I know this is completely cheesy which is fine. You can be the Mac and I can be the cheese."

I'm caught off guard when my vision blurs and a sob erupts between my lips. His eyes shoot to me and widen. "Oh, fuck! What did I do? Did I do something wrong? Please, don't cry! I'm sorry."

I shake my head as I pull the noodle out and crush it to my chest. This is the absolute sweetest thing anyone has ever done for me. I hiccup as I say, "Thank you!"

He immediately engulfs me in a hug, holding me tight as I sob. I hear his whispered words as he rocks us side to side. "It's okay, Mac. I've got you. Everything's okay."

My chest tightens at his words, which triggers me to cry harder. Nothing has ever been okay in my life. This man asked me up to his room, and I automatically thought he wanted sex. Instead, he bought me a cheesy ass gift. This amazing man will never understand what this means to me.

He continues holding me as I cry and whispers, "I've got you."

CHAPTER ELEVEN
SILAS

Huffing out a sigh, I pull on a pair of sweatpants and a tank. I rub my face and let out a groan as I make my way down the stairs. I slept like utter shit last night. She haunted every bit of my dreams, which could account for the hard-on I'm still sporting. Fucking hell, I hate my damn life. Why am I so hooked on this girl? I've never thought of wanting or needing anyone other than my brothers. I can feel my walls tremble and shake, wanting to crumble when I'm around her, but I need to stay focused. I need to remember my purpose. I am vengeance and pain. I am nothing but my beast.

Fuck. I feel like my body is saying fuck the beast though because I'm currently sporting a hard-on. One problem at a time. When was the last time I fucked a chick? Ugh, no wonder I'm horny as fuck around her. The dress she wore last night didn't help matters at all. Pausing on the stairs, I debate between going back upstairs to handle business myself or sporting a very noticeable hard-on to breakfast. If it were only my brothers here, I wouldn't hesitate to march my way downstairs with zero fucks to give. But we do have Macy here now, and I don't need her getting any ideas that she has me under her spell like she does my brothers.

Growling, I readjust myself and continue down the stairs. Fuck it. It's early in the morning; my dick should fuck all the way off by the time she comes down. Making my way over to the refrigerator, I pull out eggs and bacon.

Slapping some bacon on a skillet as well as cracking a few eggs, I begin my morning routine. I start the coffee as I grab a spatula to scramble the eggs.

I'm brought out of my morning trance when I hear soft feet pattering down the stairs. Huffing out another sigh, I try to ignore the sudden rush of my heartbeat. I hear a chair scratching against the floor, but she hasn't said a word.

I look over my shoulder to find her hiding her face as she cuddles that stupid Squishmallow Luka got her. She looks so damn tiny right now. I've seen the wolf beneath her skin. She's a wolf just like us, but she's still a cub. Not yet grown into the beast ours have become. I'm not sure if I should be proud she hasn't become a ruthless beast like us or sad that she hasn't allowed herself to become the beast needed to survive in this world.

Grabbing a plate, I serve up some eggs and bacon. Turning, I slide it toward her. "I'm not the best cook, but I can manage the basics."

Macy

I make my way down the stairs the next morning, not wanting to take the elevator. When I turn the corner, I notice Silas in the kitchen. Shit. I know my eyes are still a bit puffy from my crying fest last night, and I don't want to face the guys yet. I take a deep breath and hold my new Squishmallow to my chest. Heading to the island, I sit with my eyes downcast, not wanting to meet Silas's gaze. Suddenly, a plate is set in front of me filled with eggs and bacon.

His voice sounds gruff from sleep as he says, "I'm not the best cook, but I can manage the basics."

I look up at him and wait for him to say something in regard to how I look. I know I must look rough, considering my hair is up in a messy bun, and I'm in a band tee and sweatpants. Nothing compared to the beauty I was last night. I watch as he looks from me to the plate, then back up at me. He points to the food with the spatula. "Eat," is all he says before he turns back around to continue cooking.

I huff out a breath of relief that he didn't say anything and shove a fork full of eggs into my mouth. There's a ding from behind me, and I look over my shoulder to find Luka stepping out of the elevator. He smiles, and I immediately turn back around. I can feel my face heat in embarrassment over what happened last night. My grip on the noodle in my lap tightens as I hear his footsteps get closer.

There's a soft brush of lips on the top of my head before he sits down next to me. "Good morning."

I whisper, "Good morning." Then I shove another fork full of eggs into my mouth.

He chuckles before asking, "Do you have a plate for me too, brother?" I hear the clatter of dishes and look up when a plate is set down beside me. I look over to see Luka peering down with a smile. "Thanks, Si."

Silas grunts. "You know I hate when you call me that."

Luka snickers beside me, as he munches on a piece of bacon. "I know. You let Jane call you that all the time, though."

Silas turns a glare on Luka as he says, "And you know as well as I do that I can't make that woman do anything she doesn't want to do. She knows I hate that nickname."

Luka laughs and teases, "Which is why she does it, I'm sure."

Silas groans as he turns back to the stove. "I'm sure."

The elevator dings again, and I look over my shoulder with a piece of bacon in my mouth. Jax walks out looking a little disheveled. He takes one last drag from his cigarette before throwing it in the trash by the elevator. I've been wondering why that was there. He shoves a hand through his loose, long hair as he makes his way over to the island.

He takes a seat next to me before looking at me. He must see something in my eyes because he gives me a soft smile as he says, "You still look beautiful, by the way."

I snort as I look back down at my food. "I doubt that."

He bumps his shoulder with mine. "You are capable of looking beautiful in what you wore last night just as much as are in what you are wearing right now."

Trying to change the subject, I say, "You know, you shouldn't smoke."

"And why is that?" I can hear the laughter in his tone.

I look up at him with a raised brow. "Other than it being bad for you?"

He smirks. "Other than that."

"Well, it will kill you because of how much you smoke." I'm not really sure why I seem to care enough to say something. I've never cared about other men smoking before. But with Jax, it's like an impulse.

He shrugs. "My job will most likely kill me before the cigs do."

I frown at his words. Does he not care that he can be killed? Does he not care about dying at all? I can't stop my next words as they tumble from my lips, "Do you not care that you would leave your brothers behind?"

He looks between his brothers for a moment before looking back at me. "My brothers have accepted me for who and what I am, Mace. There are only a few who would miss me if I passed from this world."

I didn't expect his words to hit so hard. Even I'm surprised by my words as I ask, "What if I asked you to stop?"

His brow arches as he asks, "You want me to stop smoking?"

"Yes," I whisper.

His eyes take in my face before he grows serious. "And why should your request mean more than those who have asked in the past?"

He's right... Why should my request mean anything? Why do I even care? But the truth of the matter is, I do. I do care. It matters to me. "I suppose it shouldn't, but I'm asking anyway."

His gaze seems to gauge the truth of my words. He huffs out a breath and says, "Only on one condition."

I'm a bit caught off guard by the bargaining, but I go with it. "And what condition is that?"

His hazel eyes seem to swirl with emotion as he replies, "As long as you stay."

Surprised, I question, "As long as I stay?"

"I'll quit smoking for as long as you willingly stay with us." I feel like he's trying to say something more with his words. Like there is a hidden meaning behind them.

I take a deep breath. "For as long as I'm willing to stay?"

He nods. "I want you to be here because you want to be here. I want you to want to stay. I don't want you to stay because you feel like you have to or because we are paying that fuck face of a man money to keep you here."

Smirking a bit to lighten the suddenly heavy mood, I ask, "So what you're saying is you like me and want to keep me around?"

He chuckles. "I thought you would have figured that out by now." He holds out a hand as he asks, "Do we have a deal, Mace?"

I shove my fork in my mouth, reaching out and shaking his hand. He chuckles as we pull away. "You realize you could have just used your other hand instead of the one holding your fork?"

I smile as I pull the fork out of my mouth. "Noodle would have dropped to the floor if I let go."

He chuckles as he looks down to see the noodle Squishmallow in my lap. "I see. I suppose saving Noodle from crashing to the floor does take top priority."

I nod, putting another scoop of eggs in my mouth. I don't know how I've grown so comfortable with these guys so quickly, but I'm not about to analyze it right now. That's a problem for another day. I look up to find Silas looking between the three of us on the other side of the island. He has that look again. Like he's trying to figure out what's happening between his brothers and me. If he should trust me or not.

I swallow another bite of food before asking, "What's the plan for today?"

Next to me, Luka shrugs. "It's the weekend, and we don't have any other events planned."

Jax hums from beside me. "Which means it's a chill weekend!"

Chill weekend. I've never chilled before, but that sounds fun. Especially with these guys.

CHAPTER TWELVE
MACY

I've officially been here for a month, which seems crazy. That's so much money just for me to live here. None of the guys have asked for anything other than to hang out with them. Well, mostly Jax and Luka. Silas seems to be keeping his distance. He hasn't talked to me much since the night he helped me pick out my dress. He still acknowledges my presence if we are alone in a room, but otherwise, he doesn't talk with me. I don't know if that's his way of protecting himself or making sure he keeps me at a distance since this is only transactional.

The idea that I'm only a transaction hurts more than I want to admit. But the others have made sure that I've felt welcome. Luka has bought me so many stuffed animals and squishies that they take up most of the guest room. Each one he adds makes me smile. It's like a game because he just adds it to my collection, so I have to find the new one. But Noodle is still my favorite.

Jax invites me to work out with him every morning, but I told him that I don't like when people watch me work out. He smiled and said that I was welcome to chill if I wanted, so I went. He just seemed so eager for me to come with him. I felt like it was his way of asking to have a thing with me, like the stuffed animals were Luka and my thing.

The first morning I went down with him, I had brought my noodle, a mug of coffee, and my phone so I could read. Jax had asked why I read on my phone instead of an e-reader or a physical copy. I told him that I didn't want physical books for someone to destroy, and an e-reader would be easy for someone to steal. The next morning, I found a brand new e-reader on the counter by the coffee machine. I had asked about it, but Jax wouldn't fess up to buying it for me. I knew it was him though by the huge grin on his face when I squealed in excitement over it.

Now, I'm sitting against the wall of the workout room, e-reader in hand. I just downloaded a new book, and it has sucked me in. Hard. I jump when I hear Jax's voice. Looking up, I ask, "What?"

He snickers as he wipes sweat out of his eyes. "What are you reading?"

"A book." Because I have to be a smartass.

He rolls his eyes but smiles. "I assumed so, Mace. What type of book?"

I grin as I answer, "It's a romance."

He begins his cool down as he stretches in place. He starts with his arms, holding them over his head. "That's very descriptive, Mace. What is the book about?"

I huff out a sigh because I know he will continue to ask unless I tell him. "It's an Alice in Wonderland retelling."

One of his brows arches in question. "Interesting. I didn't know you could make a romance out of a fairy tale. Is it good?"

I smile as I nod. "It is so far. It's a why-choose romance. So the main female character doesn't have to choose between her love interests. There are seven guys in this story; Rab, Mor, Rook, Dee, Hatter, Arch, and Chesh. All of them are adorable with her, but I have to say I'm having a hard time choosing a favorite out of them."

Jax surprises me when he says, "Isn't that the point of a why-choose book? You don't have to choose?"

I arch a brow as I ask, "You read why-choose?"

He shrugs. "My sister loves them, so I have to listen to her talk about them a lot. It got me curious, so I've read a few."

I can't help the grin that spreads across my face. "So you're not going to get all weird about me reading them?"

He laughs. "Not at all. I find the concept of not having to choose between the people you love amazing. I think more people would be happy if they didn't feel like they had to choose between two or more people they had a connection with."

My smile turns shy. "Good to know."

Jax

I head upstairs after my workout with Macy following behind. I'm actually glad that she reads those types of books. It means she's open-minded to the idea of dating multiple guys. Learning that sent an unexpected thrill through me.

I head over to the kitchen to make my normal post-workout shake. Macy is on one of the stools behind the island, and she sets her e-reader down as she watches me navigate the kitchen. That is another thing. I love when she watches me. I can't explain why, but it makes me... happy.

I was getting jealous of her spending so much time with Luka, which is why I asked her to workout with me. I was bummed when she said she didn't like people to watch her work out, but I understood. The excitement of seeing her walk through those doors the next day had made my heart quicken. It had also made me falter in my steps as I jogged on the treadmill. Thankfully, I caught myself because eating shit in front of a beautiful woman like her would have been a major blow to my ego.

My brothers filter into the kitchen, and Luka begins breakfast while Silas sits down at the far end of the island to work on his laptop. I don't understand why Silas is distancing himself from Mace. He still buys her things. And if she mentions liking something once, he goes out and buys it for her. But whatever. The man needs to figure it out on his own; I can't help.

My phone starts ringing, and I grin when I see Jane's name across the screen. I fucking love that girl like a sister, and I am bummed that I haven't been able to see her in weeks. Jace, also known as Hades, promoted two new Hounds to take our old positions within their ranks. We are no longer Alpha and Beta for the Underworld. We are now exclusively The Steepe Brothers, and we run the Underground. Although, when we visit the compound, we still use Alpha and Beta as code names.

A smile comes over my face as I answer the phone. "Hey, Sweets!"

She giggles on the other end and says, "Hey, Jax. Can you put me on speaker? I want to talk to everyone."

I look up to find Macy looking at me in confusion. Maybe she's wondering who I'm talking to. She doesn't know about our previous jobs, but I suppose she doesn't need to. I pull the phone away and press the speaker button. "Hey, assholes! Jane's on the phone."

Her laugh echoes across the room as my brothers come closer. Luka smiles as he asks, "What's up?" Then his smile slips. "Is something wrong?"

She snorts. "What, I can't call my favorite boys just to talk?"

"We all know we're not your favorite boys," Silas replies with a smirk.

My eyes shift back to Macy to see what's going through her head. She seems curious about the dynamic between us and this woman. I see her eyes widen a bit when she notices the smirk on Silas's face. That fucker hardly ever smiles, but he smiles every time he talks to Jane.

To move the conversation along I ask, "What's up?"

I hear shuffling in the background before she says, "The guys and I wanted to invite you over for dinner. We haven't seen you in a bit, and I also have a gift for you guys."

Silas's brows knit together. "A gift? Did we miss something important?"

I can hear the smile in her voice as she answers, "No. You didn't miss anything important. It's a surprise gift!" I hear voices in the background. Then I hear her yell, "Alec! Get the fuck back here! Fucker, you knew I was on the phone."

There's some rustling and then suddenly there's a male voice. "Hello?"

I snicker. "It's us, Howe."

"Oh, that makes sense. She said she was going to call you guys to invite you over tonight. Did she tell you what time yet?"

Luka laughs. "She didn't get the chance. Alec did something to interrupt her."

Howe snickers. "The fucker knew she was on the phone and took advantage. Be here at six."

"What did he do?" Silas asks.

Howe sighs and replies, "Well... we made up this new game. And one of the rules, due to a mishap, was that we can't play when someone is on the phone."

"What was the mishap?" Luka asks. I have to admit I am curious too.

Howe sucks in a breath before saying, "Jace was on the phone with some clients and... well... we haven't heard from them in over three months."

Silas chuckles and says, "We'll be there at six." Then he must remember Macy. He lets out a sigh before adding, "We have a guest staying with us currently."

"Male or female?" Howe asks.

"Female," Silas answers, and I'm a bit sad to see his playful side shut down; the more he talks the more his smile dims.

"Associated with Hades?"

"No."

There's a pause on the other end before Howe says, "Bring her. I'm sure Jane will charm the shit out of her like she does everyone. She needs a girlfriend."

"Understood."

With a sigh, I take the phone off of the speaker. Putting it back up to my ear, I say, "See ya tonight. Tell Jane to kick Alec's ass for me."

Howe chuckles and says, "Will do." There's a click as he ends the call.

I look between my brothers. "Seems we have plans for this evening."

"And I get to meet this Jane you guys talk about all the time," Mace adds.

I'm excited for her to meet Jane. I know the two of them will instantly hit it off.

CHAPTER THIRTEEN
MACY

I have to admit that I am a bit nervous about meeting Jane. The guys talk about her often, so I know they care about her. To be honest, I am curious to meet the woman who cracked Silas's barriers. The car stops in front of a pair of tall iron gates, and Silas rolls down the window to punch in a code. Why the heck do they have so much security? Are these people a big deal? I can't imagine all this security is just because this woman is dating multiple guys. Or at least that's what I gathered from the phone call earlier.

We make it up the long drive and park in front of a huge mansion. Holy shit, this chick has it made. Maybe I need to make friends with her so I can have a rich girlfriend. You know... for when the guys stop paying for my company and all. My mood dims slightly at that thought.

As soon as the car doors slam shut, the front door of the house swings open. A female stands there framing the doorway with a wide smile. She looks like a badass, if I'm being honest. She's not slim, which is how I originally pictured her. She's curvy, at least, I assume she is, but the large hoodie she's wearing consumes her frame. For a woman, she's also tall. Her hair is a split dye; one side is a light pastel oil-slick look, and the other is a dark oil-slick look.

She waits at the door with a grin. A male's voice comes from inside, "You could have at least waited for them to make it to the door, Princess."

She glares over her shoulder as she says, "I haven't seen them in weeks! I can do whatever I want." Chuckles sound inside the house as she turns to say hello.

Luka greets her first, bending to kiss her on the cheek. "Hey, Jane."

She smiles up at him as she wraps him in a quick hug. "Hey, Luka! How's everything in the Underground?"

He chuckles as he pulls away. "Did you only invite us over to talk about work?"

Her eyes dance with amusement as she playfully slaps him on the chest. "I was only asking how everything was going."

"Everything is fine," he says as he pecks her on the cheek one last time before making his way into the house.

Jax is next as he wraps his arms around her shoulders. She giggles as she wraps her arms around his abdomen. "Hey, Jax," she mumbles between the confines of his hug.

"How are you doing, Sweets? Hope these boys are treating you right."

She grins as she pulls away. "You know my men are treating me just fine, Jax. You would be the first to know if they weren't."

He bends down, pressing a kiss to her cheek. "I better be." He squeezes past her and into the house to join Luka.

I watch as Silas makes his way over to her. She opens her arms wide as she says, "I must."

I'm a bit confused by her words until Silas chuckles, opening his arms, as he teases, "If you must." The chuckle confuses me. He never laughs. But with her, he seems more open. I'm a bit jealous, to be honest. He wraps her in a quick hug before pulling away. "I do hope I'm the one you tell first, and not my clown of a brother."

Smiling, she says, "He may act like a clown, but he's just as protective as you are."

Silas grunts. "True enough." He turns back to look at me and gestures for me to come closer. There's a slight tilt of his lips as he says, "I promise she won't bite." Jane mimes a biting motion with her teeth and then smiles.

My eyes widen at the joke, but before I can say anything, he introduces us. "This is Macy. She's staying with us for a while. I remember you saying you wanted a girlfriend." He ruffles her hair and walks into the house, leaving us to talk.

I stand there for a moment, unsure what I'm supposed to do in this situation. Jane smiles as she holds out her hand. "Hey! I'm Jane. I'll make sure to introduce you to my guys, they have horrible manners."

I walk up, grasping her outstretched hand. "I'm Macy. I'm staying with the brothers for a bit." Fucking hell, Macy. Silas just said that a few seconds ago.

She shakes my hand as she arches a brow. "For a bit?"

I nod, pulling away. "They are paying for me to stay with them. I'm an escort." Figure I should get it out there before she hears it from someone else.

She looks me up and down before looking me in the eyes. "An escort, huh? Well, you and I are going to be just fine then. Means you can destroy a man if need be." Her eyes widen as a grin spreads across her face. She reaches out, grasping my hand again, and pulls me inside. "I should show you my toys!"

I'm completely confused, but I decide to go with it. Dragging me through the house, she points to people as she walks through the living room. "Jace, Zane, Howe, and Alec. Now, we are going to have some fun before dinner."

I'm not exactly sure who was who because she pointed so fast. One of them speaks up as she drags me toward a door. "Where are you going, Princess?"

Jane looks over her shoulder. "I'm taking my new friend to see my toys, Jace."

Ah, Jace. Good to know. He looks like he is Chinese American. His eyes narrow as he says, "I thought you were going to tell the guys your news."

She huffs out a sigh as her hand stills on the handle of a door. "But..." She lifts the hand holding mine as she pouts and whines, "New friend! I want to show her my toys."

One of the other guys snickers and says, "Let her show her new friend her toys, Jace. We have all night." I realize that it's the bulky chocolate-skinned man who spoke, although I feel like that's a weird way to remember the guy. His eyes drift back to Jane as he grins. "Go have fun with your friend, Starlight."

Jane smiles as she opens the door, yelling over her shoulder, "Thanks, Howe."

Alright, two names down. Two more to go. Jane ushers me down some stairs and into what looks like a basement. She flips on a light, and my jaw drops as I take in the room. It's full of weapons. Like every weapon you could possibly think of. My eyes drift to hers, and I can't help but ask, "Who the fuck are you?"

She smiles. "The guys didn't tell you?"

I shake my head. "No. I don't think they trust me."

She walks over to the table full of knives, caressing them fondly. Her eyes meet mine as she grins. "I'm Persephone."

CHAPTER FOURTEEN
MACY

Wait... WHAT?! "You... you're Persephone?"

She smiles as she throws a dagger across the room and into a target behind me. "Yes."

Holy shit! Not gonna lie, I may have peed myself a little. This is no longer the sweet woman I met earlier. No, in front of me now is the Queen of the Underworld. "Um... okay, cool. So, not gonna lie, you are scary as fuck right now."

She laughs and says, "Good to know I've still got it." ,

"Did someone say you didn't? Because they obviously lied and are stupid."

She shrugs. "I just wanted to give you a... friendly warning."

I look over my shoulder to the knife stuck in the wall and then back at her with a raised brow. "That was a friendly warning?"

She plays with another knife as she says, "I didn't stab you, did I?"

I wring my hands nervously in front of me, not understanding what the fuck is going on. I sure as fuck am not going to argue though. "Nope." I pop the P and continue, "No, you did not."

She nods. "This is a warning not to play with the men up there. They are my brothers. They would probably be pissed if they knew that I was doing this, but they are family, and I protect my family."

I give her a salute. "Message received loud and clear. Though, I'm not planning on hurting them; I'm actually quite fond of them." I laugh and continue, "Don't tell them that."

She hums as if happy with my answer, then sets the knife down as she turns fully toward me. Leaning up against the table, she says, "My protection would include you as well. That is, if you're crazy enough to be my friend."

I snort out a laugh. "I feel like it would be stupid of me to turn down your friendship."

She shrugs as she says, "Not many women want to be my friend. Either they are too scared or too jealous."

I make my way over to lean against the table next to her, then say, "Not many women want to be my friend, either. Mainly because they are jealous."

"Yeah, I can see that." She huffs out a sigh before saying, "I suppose we should get back upstairs. Everyone is probably wondering why I've had you down here for so long. Plus, I need to give them my surprise." She grunts as she pushes off the table, then rubs at her belly.

My eyes widen as I whisper, "You're pregnant?"

She smiles as she makes her way back up the stairs. "We found out the gender last week. We did one of those blood tests so we could find out as early as possible. We wanted to wait to tell the brothers till we knew."

I can't help but smile as I follow up the stairs behind her. "That's amazing. Congratulations!"

She pauses at the top of the stairs and lets out a sigh. "Thank you. I'm a bit nervous to tell them."

I blow out a raspberry and say, "I haven't known them for long, but I know they will be excited for you."

She nods, takes a deep breath, then exhales as she opens the door. As we walk into the room, all eyes turn to us, and I'm suddenly a bit overwhelmed at being the center of attention. Jane pops out a hip and arches a brow. "What?"

One of the males, who I have yet to figure out his name, points at me. "I'm surprised she is still in one piece."

Jane snorts out a laugh as I come up behind her. I throw an arm over her shoulder in a show of friendship. She turns to me, grinning. I look back at the male who spoke. "So little faith in your girl or even my ability to fight her off?"

Jane laughs as the male's eyes widen, looking between the two of us. I think he realizes that this is a losing battle, and either way, he will offend someone. Another male steps up and says, "Alec, I would recommend shutting up now."

He turns his gaze to Jane as he says, "Didn't you want to give them your surprise, Sunshine?"

Jane claps her hands together. "Right!" I remove my arm from around her so she can do her thing. She walks over to the kitchen and pulls out three decorative bags. With a smile, she hands one to each brother. "Okay! Open them!" she says as she claps with excitement.

I watch as they pull the tissue paper out of their bags, then each pull out a tiny onesie that I'm assuming has something on it. I have to admit, it's pretty cute how all three of them immediately look back at her in sync.

Luka's the first to break the silence. "You're pregnant?"

She nods enthusiastically as she points at the bags. "There's more!"

Luka looks back in the bag and pulls out an envelope. I watch as Jax and Silas do the same. Luka rips his open first. He withdraws a card, and I try to see what it is as he opens it. He lifts up what looks like a sonogram picture, then his eyes shift back to the card. He bites his lip, reading whatever Jane wrote inside.

Luka looks up with a huge grin as he puts the card back in his bag before softly setting it on the ground. Rushing over to Jane, he wraps her in a huge hug. "You're having a little girl!"

She laughs as she cries, "Yes!"

He pulls away, smiling down at her. I can see the glassy sheen in his eyes as he says, "I would be honored to be her uncle." Pressing a kiss to her forehead, he pulls away. He barely has a chance to move out of the way before Jax is in his place.

Holding a hand out in front of her belly, he looks up at her and asks, "May I?"

She grins as she nods. "Of course!"

He kneels on the ground, so his face is in front of her belly, then places his palm on her stomach with a laugh. "I have no idea how we missed this belly."

She laughs as she tangles her fingers in his long hair. She ruffles it a bit as she says, "Well, I've been wearing baggy clothes for a reason."

His eyes are locked on her abdomen as he gently caresses her belly with his palm. When I see tears sliding down his face, I'm shocked to see that he has a huge grin. Softly, he says, "Hey, little baby sweets. You have no idea how much you are already loved. You have some fierce protectors out here, so be ready." He presses a soft kiss to her belly before standing up and wrapping his arms around her in a soft hug. "I'm so happy for you, Sweets."

Jane hugs him back before pulling away. She wipes at her own face as she gives him a watery smile. "She's so lucky to have you as an uncle."

He grins down at her as he wipes a thumb across her cheeks. "I think I'm the lucky one." He presses a kiss to her forehead like his brother before him, then steps away.

I look over to Silas to see his reaction, but he's still staring down at the card. His body is stiff, but I can tell that he's holding the card gently. I turn when I hear Jane's soft voice, "Si?"

It's like he's shocked back to reality. His body jerks, and he's suddenly rushing toward Jane. I feel the sudden urge to intervene and protect her, considering how fast he's moving, but when I look over and see her smiling, I stop myself. She's known these men longer than I have.

He ensnares her in a hug, and I'm standing close enough that I can hear his whispered words, "I don't deserve this honor."

His words confuse me until Jane whispers, "You deserve so much more than this, Si. Please do me the honor of being her godfather. I know that no one will protect her more fiercely than you. If anything were to ever happen to me and the guys…"

"Don't say that," Silas demands.

Jane pulls back enough to look up at him. "Please, Silas?"

He looks down at her, his glassy eyes, before nodding. "Of course, I will."

She grins up at him as she says, "I love you, grumpy head."

I watch a smirk cross his lips as he whispers, "I love you, too. Even if you are a handful of a sister."

She laughs as she playfully pushes him. "I'm an amazing sister!"

He snorts. "I don't have anything to compare you to, so I'll take your word for it."

She gives him one last hug before pulling away. "Let's eat!"

Jax lets out a yip and yells, "It's time to celebrate!"

I stay where I am for a moment, taking in everything. I watch as Jane makes her way over to Jace, giving him a quick kiss before taking a seat. I watch as her other males surround her, smothering her in kisses and asking what she wants to eat. Jax and Silas make their way over to the kitchen area, and Jax slaps Zane, I think, on the back with a laugh. I see Silas do the same with Jace.

I sigh. This right here, is something I wish I had. They act like a family even though they aren't related.

Luka bumps my shoulder, and I jump, startled. "You okay?" he asks.

I nod. "Yeah, of course."

He arches a brow, but doesn't call me on my lie, just holds out a hand for me to take. "Let's go join the others."

I look down at his hand for a moment before slipping mine inside his. I want this so much. I want somewhere to belong. I... I want a home. I want a family. Something that looks a lot like this...

CHAPTER FIFTEEN
MACY

I had to do a re-read of *Meddling with Madness*. There's this part where the twins, Rook and Dee, fuck Alyce at the same time. I probably should have thought about reading it in my room instead of in the workout room with Jax, though. I look up when I hear a grunt and see Jax pummeling the heavy bag with a little more vigor than before.

I snicker to myself as I ask, "Doing okay over there, Jax?"

"Fine," he says with another grunt.

I laugh as I set my book down. "What's wrong?"

"Nothing."

"Jax?" I wait until he huffs out a sigh, then bangs his head against the bag. "What's wrong?"

"You really don't want to know," he mumbles.

"I really do. So spill."

He huffs out another sigh as he lightly punches the bag with his glove. "So there's this girl who I like."

My heart stops. Slow the fuck down, Macy, he's probably not talking about you. I hum before saying, "Oh? And what seems to be the issue?"

He punches the bag again. "I don't think she likes me. And even if she does, my brother likes her too. I don't know if she would be okay dating us both."

My heartbeat starts to quicken as I bite my lip and play along. "Have you asked her yet?"

He shakes his head, so I ask, "Why not?"

He stops and rests his head against the bag. "To be honest, I'm nervous."

"Nervous? I find it hard to believe that a playboy like you would be scared to ask a girl if she likes you."

He snorts. "Well, other girls never made my gut feel like it had trapped thousands of butterflies."

Holy fucking shit, that's the sweetest thing I've ever heard! "Well, what if she said she liked you first?"

He turns his face enough to look at me, then huffs out a breath before answering, "Well, I'd ask if she minds that my brother also likes her and that we both want to be with her."

I give him a shy smile as I say, "Well, I suppose his brother would have to ask if I liked him too. Even though I may like his brother."

He pushes away from the punching bag and walks toward me, holding out a hand to help me up from the ground. He doesn't let go as I get to my feet in front of him. His chest is right in front of my face, and all I can say is... yum. It's smooth and glistens from his workout. I just want to... My face flames at the direction my thoughts take, and my gaze shoots up to meet his.

He looks down at me with hunger in his eyes as he asks, "What if he wanted to kiss her?"

My voice sounds breathy as I say, "You should do it and find out."

His hand sneaks up between us to cup my face as he slowly lowers his lips to mine. At first the kiss is soft, but then it changes as I press myself closer to him.

His grip on my face tightens as he walks me backward and pushes me up against the wall. I groan into his mouth before we separate, both of us panting. His eyes search mine before he says, "I like you a lot, Mace."

"I like you, too, Jax."

He presses his lips back to mine, and I let out a groan as I wrap my arms around his neck. He growls as he presses his hard dick into my abdomen.

Panting, he pulls away. "Fucking hell, Mace! I want you so much."

Humming in agreement, I say, "I'm fine with that." I move to kiss him again, but he stops me.

"I don't want you to think this is part of the job. I want you, Mace. Not Macy the Escort, but you."

I bite my lip, trying to fight back the wave of emotion his words bring. With a nod, I say, "I'd like that a lot."

He grins down at me as he takes my hand. "Let's go."

I laugh when he tries to tug me away. "Where are we going?"

He looks back at me and says, "To take a shower. I stink."

I shake my head, pulling him back. "You don't need to take a shower."

Looking down at himself, he looks back up at me with an arched brow. "But I stink."

Rolling my eyes, I tug him, and he steps back toward me. Without much thought, I run my tongue up the center of his chest like I've been fantasizing about doing. With a raised brow, I look back up and tease, "Convinced now?"

"Fuck yeah." He pushes me back up against the wall, smashing his lips to mine hungrily.

I slide my hands up his back, then run my nails back down.

With a growl, he slips his hands under my ass and lifts me up. He pushes his body into mine as he shifts his hands under my booty shorts. His fingers slide up under my underwear, gripping my ass.

I wrap my arms around his neck and weave my fingers through his hair.

He pulls away, panting as he turns from the wall, still holding me. "Where are we going now?" I ask with a laugh.

"Somewhere I can properly fuck you."

I laugh again as he jogs as best he can while carrying me to the room next to the gym. I look around, finding a couch and a recliner. He sets me on the couch before kneeling in front of me.

With a grin, he slips his fingers under the hem of my shorts. "You mind?"

I shake my head, lifting my butt enough for him to slip off my shorts and underwear. Before I can ask what he's doing, he slides an arm under each of my thighs, sliding me forward. His mouth meets my sex, and I groan, falling back. He sucks on my clit before shoving his tongue inside my cunt. My hands come up, tangling in his hair, which is somehow still in a messy bun. He hums and my thighs tighten around his head.

Fucking hell, I can't remember the last time a guy used his mouth on me. With my thighs more on his shoulders now, he manages to slip a finger inside me as he shifts his mouth to my clit. He moves his finger tauntingly slow, and I whine. He adds another finger as he increases his pace, then finds just the right spot to make me cry out in pleasure.

I'm panting as I grip his hair tighter. "Don't you dare fucking stop!" In the next instant, he hits a spot just right with his fingers as he sucks my clit and hums.

I come with a scream. I'm panting and delirious with pleasure as Jax slips his fingers out. He smiles up at me, then sucks his fingers into his mouth. He hums as he stands.

I can make out his extremely hard cock in his basketball shorts.

I grin up at him. "My turn."

He smirks and pulls his shorts down. Well, it seems he had absolutely nothing on under there. His cock stands tall and proud. Can't blame the fella I suppose, but holy shit, is he impressive. I would know. I've seen A LOT of cocks, though I've got to say, I haven't seen any quite as impressive as his.

"Mace, you have to say something because you staring at my dick is giving me a complex over here."

I snort out a laugh. "Sorry, I was just admiring."

He looks down at himself and then back up at me with a raised brow. "Do I even want to know?"

I roll my eyes as I stand from the couch and rip my shirt over my head, then do the same with my bra. His eyes drop to my chest. I grin when I see them darken with hunger. "Do I want to know?" I parrot back. Let's be honest, he's probably been with just as many women as I have men. A girl can get a complex, too, but I'm not going to let him know that.

His eyes meet mine before he rushes me. I let out a squeak as his hands grip my hips tightly. He does an impressive lift, then twists as he falls onto the couch with me in his arms. He grunts but manages to keep me suspended in the air, so I don't crush his dick.

He sets me onto his lap, and my clit rubs against his cock. I wrap my arms around his neck, so I can slide my fingers through his hair. Slipping my fingers under the hair tie, I pull. Surprisingly, the tie doesn't get caught, and his long, wavy hair falls.

He smiles up at me. "Most women hate my hair being down."

With a grin, I tangle my fingers through the strands. I tug a bit, and he growls. "I love it." I smash my lips to his as I rub my clit against his cock. He moans as his fingers dig into my hips. I nip at his bottom lip before pulling away.

"Fucking hell woman, I won't last long if you keep humping me like that," he says as he pants.

"I suppose you should fuck me then."

He shakes his head. "I want you to ride me."

I raise a brow in question. Most men hate when I'm in control. "You want me to ride you?"

He gives me a dark grin as he says, "Like a fucking Goddess."

I smile and raise myself enough to position his cock at my entrance. I'm already wet from my previous orgasm, and I know I'm fucking slick with arousal as well. My eyes meet his. "Then a Goddess I shall be," I say as I impale myself with his cock in one quick motion until he's balls deep inside me.

His fingers grip my thighs tight as he groans my name. "Macy."

The way he says my name shatters my need to go slow, and I begin to fuck him in earnest. Raising myself and slamming down so he hits just the right spot. He doesn't move as I fuck him, allowing me full control. I can tell it's taking everything in him to remain still, though, by the death grip he has on my thighs.

He's biting his lip with his head thumping the back of the couch, his fingers turning white with his grip on me. He releases his lip as he pants out, "Mace, you have to come."

"Why's that?" I pant back.

He groans before saying, "I'm not going to make it much longer with the way your cunt is gripping my cock."

I let out a breathy laugh. "Then come."

He shakes his head, eyes squeezed shut in concentration. "A woman should come as many times as possible before a man does."

"I've already come once, Jax."

"Not enough," he moans. His eyes open lazily as one of his hands snakes between us and finds my clit. He rubs it in time with each of my thrusts.

I moan and lean forward to press my lips against his. He devours my mouth as he rubs my clit, then presses down hard. I scream into his mouth as I come around him.

He growls and continues rubbing my clit. He forgets about letting me fuck him as he uses his other hand on my hip to press me down onto him while using the couch as leverage to thrust upward.

My fingers tug on his hair as we devour each other's mouths. He thrusts upward, hitting just the right spot as he presses down on my clit again. I break away from his mouth as we both come, me screaming his name as he howls mine. He holds me against him as my cunt pulses around his cock.

Still breathing heavily, he says, "I think we may need a shower now."

I chuckle as I pull away to look into his eyes. I wasn't expecting to see happiness there. He's happy being with me. I can't stop myself as I press my lips to his softly. His lips move slowly against mine, keeping us connected.

I pull away and close my eyes, resting my forehead against his. "Thank you," I whisper.

His fingers make slow circles on my thighs as he whispers, "For what?"

Trying to hold back the emotion clogging my throat, I press my lips to his again. I've never had a moment like this with a guy, and it's fucking scary. This is scaring the shit out of me. I pull away again, looking down at him.

He must see something in my eyes because he gives me a soft smile and reaches up, cupping my face in his palm. His thumb caresses my cheek as he whispers, "You're Mace with me. My Mace."

I squeeze my eyes shut, trying to hold back tears. Leaning forward, I press my lips to his. If I cry right now, it will ruin the moment. This beautiful moment I'm sharing with this amazing man. I don't want it ruined, so I continue kissing him, hoping to show him just how much his words mean to me.

CHAPTER SIXTEEN
Macy

I wake up engulfed in a warm body, and I can't suppress a sigh as I curl closer. It's been a week since Jax told me he liked me, and ever since then, he has been snuggly. Taking every opportunity to hold or cuddle me. He snuck into my room last night, and I had expected him to want sex, but he just nuzzled in close behind me and instantly fell asleep. I'm not saying sex hasn't happened in the past week. It has. Usually after his workouts or in the shower.

I've been waiting for Luka to say something, but he hasn't. He's actually been quiet, which makes me question Jax's words. Does Luka really want to be with me too?

Jax's arms tighten around me as he huffs out a breath. I laugh and say, "Morning."

He hums. "Morning, Mace," he replies, his voice still rough from sleep.

"Did you sleep well?"

He snuggles closer and presses a kiss to my shoulder. "Like a rock. You?" I hum in response. After another kiss to my shoulder, he asks, "Are you ready for today?"

Furrowing my brows in confusion, I ask, "Today?"

He nods. "Yeah. Didn't... oh shit!"

"What?" I ask, squeezing his arm that is wrapped around my abdomen.

He groans. "It was supposed to be a surprise."

"What—" before I can finish asking my question, there's a knock at my door.

"Mac, can I come in?" Luka asks from the other side.

"Come in," Jax calls out before I can say anything. I try to pull myself out of his arms, but he has a death grip on me.

"Jax!" I reprimand.

Luka opens the door, peeking around the corner. "Am I interrupting something?"

I expected him to be upset that he found Jax in my bed, but he seems more concerned that he may have interrupted us. I push myself up as much as Jax allows and shake my head. "No, not at all. What's up?"

He makes his way further into the room, closing the door behind him. His eyes stay on mine, which is impressive considering I'm only in my sports bra and underwear. Seemingly nervous, he says, "I wanted to ask you something."

I smile as I say, "Okay..."

He looks down, scuffing his foot across the floor before looking back up at me. "Will you go on a date with me?"

My eyes widen. A date? I've never been on a date before. Unless you count the dozens of times I've *been* someone's date. "You... Want to go on a date? With me?"

He nods, his cheeks turning pink. "Yes," he whispers.

I'm silent for a moment, taken aback at the concept of someone wanting to go on a date with me. But he must take my silence as me declining his offer because he lets out a self-deprecating laugh and says, "Or not, that's fine. I just thought..."

"No!" I yell, jumping away from Jax.

Luka flinches as he looks back at me, eyes wide. "No?"

"That's not what I meant." Facepalming, I groan. With a sigh, I look back up at him and smile. "I would love to go on a date with you."

He gives me a hopeful smile. "Really?"

I nod. "Yes!"

The smile he gives me puts his dimples on full display. "Sweet!" He claps his hands together before letting his eyes drift over my body. I watch his throat bob as his eyes meet mine again. "I'll just... let you get dressed." He turns quickly and runs right into the door.

I can't stop the laugh that bubbles up as I ask, "Are you okay?"

"Fucking hell... Shit." He turns to face me with bright red cheeks. "Fine. Can't say the same for my pride," he mumbles as he closes the door behind him.

Jax roars with laughter as I turn toward him on the bed and swat at him playfully. "Stop!"

He snorts and says, "Oh my god, that was hilarious."

I shake my head, smiling. "He was nervous." Jax laughs even harder, and I swat him with a pillow.

Wiping his eyes, he says with a laugh, "I've never seen my brother so nervous around a girl in my life."

I arch a brow. "Really?"

He nods as he pushes himself off the bed, stretching then making his way toward my bathroom. "He likes you."

Wondering where he's going, I ask, "What are you doing?"

He looks over his shoulder before disappearing around the corner. "I'm going to help you pick out a date outfit. I know where he's taking you, so I figured I would help."

I jump off the bed. "Yes, please!"

Looking at myself in the mirror, I take a deep breath. Why am I so nervous? It is just a date. Ugh, who am I kidding? I've never been on a date, and I am seriously freaking out.

Jax comes up behind me and meets my gaze in the reflection. He arches a brow and asks, "Why do you look like you're about to vomit?"

I shake my head. "I'm fine."

He rolls his eyes as he moves closer to wrap his arms around me. Caging me in as his arms cross over my chest, he pulls me into his warm embrace. He presses a kiss to the top of my head before saying, "I can tell you're not fine. What's wrong?"

I shrug. "I don't know. I guess, I'm nervous."

He smirks. "It's Luka, there's nothing to be nervous about."

Huffing out a sigh, I say, "I've never been on a date before. What do I even do?"

Releasing his hold on me, he turns me around to face him. He smiles and cups my face in his palms. "You have fun. That's all. Just enjoy your time with Luka."

I puff out my cheeks, holding my breath for a moment before I blow it out in a huff. I nod. "Okay."

He presses a soft kiss to my nose before pulling away. "You look beautiful."

I look down at myself before looking back up at him. With an arched brow, I say, "I'm in a pair of jeans and a band t-shirt."

He snorts, then says, "I think you underestimate how good you look in a pair of curve-hugging jeans."

With a roll of my eyes, I slip into the black army boots he picked out, along with a leather jacket. I do a twirl and look up at him with a smirk. "So, I look okay for the date?"

He lifts his fist to his mouth and exaggerates biting it while he hums. "If you weren't going on a date with my brother, I would be taking you out myself."

I snort but feel my cheeks heat at the compliment. "Thank you."

He shakes himself before saying, "Wear your hair in a low ponytail till you get where you're going. Otherwise, you're ready for your date." He taps the door frame and says, "I'll meet you downstairs, Mace."

I nod as I turn back to the mirror and braid my hair into a low pony. Looking over myself one last time, I give myself a nod. I leave my room, making my way down the stairs instead of using the elevator. I turn the corner just in time to see Luka slipping into a leather jacket.

I pause mid-step because, damn! That man looks sexy. He's in black army boots, dark-wash jeans, and a black t-shirt. He settles his jacket in place before reaching over the chair next to him and lifting up a helmet. I'm able to finally tear my gaze from him and look toward the kitchen.

Jax is grinning as he says something to Luka. Luka only nods, then looks down at the helmet. Silas is standing there quietly, staring at Luka with pinched brows. I wonder what he's worried about.

Not wanting to feel like a weirdo standing there watching them, I begin walking toward Luka. "What's the helmet for?" I ask.

All the guys turn to look in my direction. My eyes are on Luka as I watch him take in my outfit. His eyes widen before his throat bobs, and his eyes meet mine. "Hey," his voice squeaks out. He clears his throat before saying, "Hey, Mac. You look amazing."

I smile as I say, "You don't look bad yourself."

With a smile, he holds the helmet out to me. "It's part of the surprise."

I arch a brow as I take the helmet. He grabs his, then takes my hand, leading me to the elevator with a grin. "I hope you like it."

I squeeze his hand as I ask, "Like what?"

He smirks and replies, "You'll see."

I grin as I look over my shoulder and yell, "Bye!"

Jax gives me a wave as he snickers, then says, "You kids have fun."

I snort out a laugh as I look in Silas's direction. He gives me a nod before saying, "Be safe."

Giving him a smile, I nod back. "Will do." I bump Luka's shoulder as we enter the elevator. "You wouldn't let anything happen to me, would you, Cheesy man?"

With a grin, he replies, "Never, Mac."

CHAPTER SEVENTEEN

MACY

When we exit the elevator into the garage, I'm speechless. "Is... Is that a motorcycle?"

He steps away from me with a wide grin as he says, "Yep! She's a beauty isn't she?"

Shaking myself, I laugh. "That she is."

"That's not even the best part. Watch." He moves over to the sleek black motorcycle, then presses a button. The bike suddenly begins to glow dark blue. He pats the seat before saying, "She's a Suzuki GSX-R1000R. My first girl, so I had to make her look pretty."

"Well, I don't know much about motorcycles, but I can agree she's beautiful."

He straddles the bike before sitting up and putting his helmet on. I can see the laughter in his eyes as he points at me, then the seat behind him. "Get that helmet on, Mac. Let's start this date."

Taking a deep breath, I slip the helmet on my head and make my way over. I look at the bike and then at him. "Not sure how I'm supposed to get on, Cheese man."

He huffs out a laugh. "Put one hand on my shoulder, then put your left foot on the small pedal behind my thigh and swing the opposite leg over."

I look down to find the pedal he's talking about. Resting a hand on his shoulder, I do as instructed. Once I'm seated on the tiny seat behind him, I situate myself.

"Alright, you are going to be my backpack."

"Your backpack?"

He reaches for my hand, wrapping it around him. "Wrap your arms around me, and scoot as close as you can to my back. Hold on tight like you're a backpack."

Doing as instructed, I hold on as tight as I can. He chuckles and says, "Now, if you need me to stop or anything just tap my thigh or chest. I won't be able to hear you once we get moving. You can loosen your grip whenever you feel comfortable. Lean into the curves. I won't go too fast since it's your first time."

I nod against his back as my nerves begin to build. He pats my hand as he says, "Don't worry. I won't let anything happen to you."

He removes his hand from mine and starts the motorcycle. The vibrations surprise me, and I let out a squeak. He laughs as he slowly maneuvers the bike around until we face the exit. Over the roar that echoes loudly in the garage, I hear him yell, "Here we go!"

I squeeze a little tighter against him, and he gives the bike a bit more gas as we exit into the star-filled night. It takes a few minutes for me to get a feel of how I need to move and to feel comfortable enough to loosen my grip on him.

As we drive through the city, I look around. The neon lights blur as we speed by. I have to say, this is a different view of the city. Usually, I'm behind tinted windows while riding past the stores. I would be able to look into each storefront with no issue, but on the back of the bike, everything is blurred.

A laugh slips out as I take in the sights. I feel his hand wrap around my calf, giving it a gentle squeeze before returning it to the controls. I give his chest a gentle tap. I can feel his laugh as he gives my fingers a gentle squeeze in return.

The moment we leave city limits, it's like we have entered into a completely different world. We are surrounded by darkness. Our single headlight is the only thing guiding us through the inky black night.

There aren't many people who head out here anymore, this long-forgotten world of rolling hills. I gasp as I look up to the sky. Stars. So many stars. The city lights don't reach this far out to swallow up their soft glow. Tightening my grip on Luka with my thighs, I reach up toward the sky. As if I could capture their beauty, I grasp toward the stars themselves.

I feel so free in this moment. Letting my eyes close, I lift my arms out to my sides, feeling the breeze as it whips past me.

The feel of the bike slowing has me opening my eyes to find us coming upon an area decorated with string lights. As we get closer, I see a large parked truck that is strung with fairy lights.

I have to hold back a squeal of excitement as Luka turns into the small graveled area, and the whole picture of our date comes into view. Once we are parked, I struggle not to fall off the back of the bike as I try to get off as fast as possible. Pulling my helmet off, I take a look around.

The truck strung with dim fairy lights is full of blankets and pillows. There's a blanket spread out on the ground that has a basket with a few pillows. I have never felt as excited and happy as I do at this moment.

I turn to find Luka with his helmet off, rubbing the back of his neck with a shy smile. "So... how did I do?"

I let out a squeal as I run at him, then jump. He catches me with a laugh. Smashing my lips to his, I wrap my arms around his neck. He hums as he moves his grip from my waist to my thighs to hold me up.

We break away, panting. With a smirk, he asks, "So I'm going to take that as a, 'you did great, Luka.'"

I laugh and give him a quick peck on the lips. "You did amazing! I've never had anyone do something like this for me."

Smiling, he lowers me back down to the ground and slips his hand into mine. "Well, you deserve the best, Mac. Now, let's eat."

Looking around, I'm still in awe, but I can't deny that I'm hungry. "Sounds perfect." A little too perfect if I am being honest. The old me would have run away right about now due to how perfect this moment is. But I really like these guys, and against my better judgment, I am going to enjoy this. I am going to enjoy whatever moments these guys provide me with because I know at some point it's going to end. All good things end eventually.

I'm pulled out of my thoughts when Luka asks, "So I'm assuming you have been on dates before. Can't imagine a single person not wanting to go on a date with you." He tugs me over to the truck and jumps into the back, holding a hand outstretched to me.

With ease, he pulls me into the truck bed alongside him, and we make ourselves comfortable on the mounds of pillows and blankets. He pulls out a basket, then turns to me and begins plating several bits of finger food. I arch a brow. He hands me the plate as I ask, "Do men who pay me to go with them to events so they aren't alone count as dates?"

His brows knit together. "I don't think that would be considered a date, more like a job."

I shrug as I bite into a strawberry. Humming in satisfaction at the sweet taste, I say, "Then no, I've never been on a date before."

Luka huffs out a sigh. "Well, I'm suddenly ten times more nervous about this evening."

I laugh as I pat his knee. "You are doing great so far. No complaints at all."

He takes a deep breath before saying, "I suppose that means you've never been asked the 'first date' questions."

I shake my head as I continue to eat the delicious food. He taps his chin for a moment before popping a strawberry into his mouth. After a moment, he snaps his fingers. "Got one!"

I jump at the suddenness, letting out a light laugh as he scoots a bit closer. "Got one?"

He nods. "I thought of a question. I hate the typical questions people ask."

"Like what?"

"Well, usually people ask easy questions like, what's your favorite color?"

I grin. "I didn't realize that was a typical question. Do you not want to know my favorite color?"

He smirks as he says, "It's blue. Well, sapphire blue."

My eyes widen in surprise. "How did you figure that out?"

With a shrug, he says, "I noticed that it was the color you gravitated toward when we went shopping. But you don't have many things in that color. What you do have in that color, you don't wear very often, unlike the things in black or red."

My head tilts a bit as I take him in. My brows knit as I ask, "Wouldn't that imply my favorite color is black or red?"

He points at my face as he says, "It's in your eyes. You look at the color blue like it's a new book. Your face lights up." He pops a grape in his mouth before continuing. "You should wear the color more, if you like it so much."

I look down, picking at the blankets under me. Shrugging, I say, "I suppose I never wanted to wear it because it was my color. I didn't want to share it with anyone else."

"Your clients," he says softly.

I look up, expecting to find judgment in his eyes, but I find only understanding. There's also a bit of sadness as he huffs out a breath and says, "If you don't want to wear the color around the house, I completely understand. It's hard to have something that's only yours, especially in your line of work."

I nod as I feel a tightness in my chest. I've never had someone understand that in my line of work, it feels like everyone gets a piece of you. It's not often that you have something that is yours and only yours.

He places a hand on my knee, his thumb softly stroking my leg. My eyes meet his, and he smiles softly. "My favorite color is green."

I laugh as the seriousness of the conversation lifts. "There are many shades of green."

He laughs. Grinning at me, he says, "Lime green."

Humming, I nod. "That seems like a Luka color. Very bright and fun."

He gives my knee a light squeeze before moving it behind him to lean back. With a shrug, he says, "It's a fun color."

I lean back as well as I say, "You never asked me what you wanted to."

"Right! Well, I was going to ask what your dream place would be like? If you had no restrictions."

"Dream place? Like a house?"

He shrugs. "Dream house or bedroom. Whatever you want."

That is definitely not a question I've ever been asked before. It takes me a few moments to think about my answer. "I suppose I would want a place like yours. Something with a lot of windows, so I could see the city all around me. My bedroom would have a dream-like bed with lots of pillows and blankets. I want a bookshelf that takes up a whole wall, so I can get all the books I want. Also, a reading nook with a hammock and fluffy blankets to keep me cozy."

I pause when I notice Luka watching me with a soft smile. Embarrassed by my answer, I rub the back of my neck. "What?"

He shakes his head, still smiling. "Nothing. Keep going."

I shake my head. "You don't want to hear the rest. It's stupid anyway."

He moves closer to me and hooks his finger under my chin, lifting my face. My eyes meet his as he says, "I want to hear. Keep going." He presses a soft kiss to my lips before slipping his fingers between mine. He tugs me to one edge of the truck bed and pulls me into his lap.

Resting his chin on my shoulder, he repeats, "Keep going."

The butterflies in my stomach are intense as I clear my throat to continue. My reply comes out a bit too high-pitched for my liking when I reply, "Okay."

His chuckle vibrates against my back. "Go on then, Mac."

So, I continue telling him about my dream room. Which includes every stuffed animal he's given me, along with the few books Jax bought me. I want a small storage area for my favorite snacks, as well as an en-suite bathroom that is all my own.

Luka added that the floors should be heated so my tiny toes wouldn't get cold. He said that there needs to be a drawer full of socks anyways. I think he only wants the drawer of socks so he can buy me the ones with the cat paws on the bottom. I'm not going to complain though, I think the idea is cute.

Silas

Tonight was a mistake. I shouldn't have allowed them out on a date. I know exactly how Luka is when it comes to dating. The lengths he will go if he really likes a girl. Grunting, I punch the heavy bag again as it swings back.

Maybe the gym was a mistake too. Jax knows me too well. I'm stressed as fuck, and when I'm stressed, I come down to the gym and work off some steam. I could play it off by saying that I've been working on a stressful deal. That the club we've been working on for Jane is causing issues. But he would see right through that in a minute. There isn't much that stresses me out anymore.

This girl, no, woman. This woman has me too much in my head. I've been thinking too much about her rather than what I should be thinking about. Too much time spent worrying about how my brothers are getting too close to her. How if she infiltrates our close knit bond, it would ruin us like it did Grayson.

Trusting a woman has led to nothing but heartache for our family. We don't know the first thing about her. We don't know why she's working the job she is, even though she has the potential to do much better for herself.

We need to know her reason for working for Marvin. No woman would happily work for that man. Most of the women we talk to try and keep as much distance from him as possible. But with her, it seems like he has a leash on her, and I want to know why.

I hit the bag one more time before I sigh. Holding onto either side of the bag, I rest my forehead against it as I breathe heavily. The fact that I know her favorite snack doesn't help us at all. I know what her favorite color is and what types of books she loves. I know that her eyes light up when she sees food, and she does a little dance as she eats.

Thumping my forehead against the bag again, I groan. "Why are you stuck in my head?"

We need to get out of the house. We need to put ourselves in an environment where she isn't the only woman around. The grand opening for Persephone's club, Asphodel, is scheduled in a few days. I could pitch the idea of a club night and invite the Underworld crew. That way Jane could steal her away for dancing, and my brothers and I could finally get some space.

Maybe if they are around other women, they will realize how bad of an idea it is to keep this one in our lives. It shouldn't be too hard to convince Jax to go clubbing. Luka hasn't enjoyed the club life much after his stint working undercover years ago, but he wouldn't be there as a manager, only for fun. Plus, Macy going would be enough to convince him to come along with Jane being there.

Thumping my head against the bag one last time, I back away, ripping my gloves off. Walking over to the bench, I grab my phone. I scroll to Jane's name and press the call button. I knew she would be at the Underworld compound, so it doesn't surprise me when she answers using my code name.

"Hey, Alpha man."

I can't help but smile as I reply, "Hey Seph. I have a question for you."

"Alright, hit me."

"Asphodel should be opening up this weekend. Do you want to do a group night to celebrate?"

There's a pause on the other end before I hear her squeal. I pull the phone away until I hear her say, "I am totally down for a club night! I want to have some fun before I get too fat."

I chuckle. "I think that's part of being pregnant, darling."

She hums. "That's what I've been told. So who will be coming?"

"I assume your boys, Beta, Apollo, Mac, and I."

"You need to give her a code name if she will be around us, Alpha. Especially since we will be going as official members of the Underworld."

I groan. "Yes, I suppose you're right."

She laughs. "I'm always right."

"Very well. I'll come up with a code name for her."

A door closes on the other end before I hear her whisper, "What's wrong, Si?"

"Nothing." I sigh, realizing I may have answered too quickly. Jane has always had a way of being able to read me. Too well for my liking.

She hums as she says, "Yeah, I know you're lying, but I'll let it slide for now. Don't fuck this up, Silas. I know how you are. You start to self-sabotage when things seem to be going too well or something seems too good to be true."

With my back against the wall, I slide down until my butt hits the ground. "What is going so well in my life that I would self-sabotage, Jane?"

She tuts at me. "I see how all three of you look at that girl. I'm not fucking blind. Don't fuck it up because you're scared. Not all women are like the one who fucked over your brother."

"I know," I whisper.

"I don't think you do. There's a difference between saying you know and believing you do. My relationship with you is entirely different from the one you have with Macy. She has the ability to break through the rough exterior you put up for everyone else." She sighs and adds quietly, "Don't fuck it up because you're afraid."

My silence must be answer enough because she huffs out a breath. "I love you, Silas."

"Yeah, you too."

She laughs lightly. "I'll see you in a few days. I better see a smile on that grizzly face of yours."

"Good luck with that."

The line clicks off, and I'm surrounded by silence. Suddenly, it feels like too much. Rising from the ground, I take the elevator to my room, not wanting to run into anyone. I need a shower and to spend some time alone, so I can rebuild my walls again before I have to face Macy.

CHAPTER EIGHTEEN
MACY

The contentment I felt after last night's date and being wrapped up in Luka's arms all evening has me in a daze until I hear Silas. I shake myself, trying to understand what he said. "What?"

His smirk is barely there, but I can make it out as he repeats himself. "I said, I made plans for this evening."

After I shovel a bite of eggs into my mouth, I point my fork at him and mumble around the food, "You made plans?"

He arches a brow as he asks, "Am I not allowed to make plans?"

I hold both hands up, surrendering. "Didn't say you couldn't make plans. This just seems more like something Jax would come up with, that's all."

Jax bumps my shoulder as he steals a piece of bacon off my plate. "What's that supposed to mean, Mace?"

I reach for the stolen bacon, but he shoves it into his mouth with a smirk. I give him a mock glare before grabbing the rest of my bacon and shoving it all in my mouth before he can steal it. Well... that was a mistake. That was too much bacon at once.

He lets out a bellowing laugh as he gets up to grab more from the other side of the island. "You didn't need to shove all six pieces in your mouth at once. I wasn't going to steal any more."

Luka gives me a concerned look as I try to chew. "You can spit them out, Mac."

I shake my head, refusing to accept defeat. I can do this. If I can fit a dick in my mouth, six pieces of bacon shouldn't be too hard. When I look up, I find Silas looking at me with an arched brow. I can tell he's trying hard not to smirk at my antics.

His eyes glisten with laughter as he says, "I think she may have too much meat in her mouth."

Bits of bacon fly out of my mouth as I explode with laughter but immediately begin coughing when a bit of bacon goes down the wrong pipe. Luka starts patting me on the back as my eyes water.

Silas snorts and says, "Seems she had too much meat at once. You should work on that."

Jax roars with laughter as he holds out a glass of water. "Here, Mace, take a drink."

I grab the glass and guzzle down a few gulps before taking a deep breath.

Jax pats my back a moment before asking, "You okay now, Sweets?"

I watch as Silas stiffens. No one else seems to notice it, but I can tell that Jax's words have bothered him. My eyes meet Silas's. They seem to have darkened when he looked at Jax before his eyes switched to meet mine. He noticed that I've been watching him.

Shrugging a bit, he goes back to the playful Silas he was earlier. "Why do you think Jax was the one to make these plans?"

I wait a moment to see if his mood switches back, but he only arches his brow, waiting for me to reply. Clearing my throat, I say, "Jax seems more like the one to make a night out at the club a thing."

Silas shrugs as he says, "I want to check out the new investment we put so much money into. Figured a night out was needed for all of us. He knocks his knuckles against the marble top island, then continues, "I invited the Underworld crew to join us. Jane said we need to come up with a name for Macy."

"Like a code name?" Luka asks.

Silas nods. "Since we will be going out with them as their Underworld personas, she said Macy needed one as well."

"It needs to go with the Greek theme," Jax adds.

Silas shrugs. "It's whatever we want or I suppose whatever she wants."

All three males' eyes shift to me, and I feel my cheeks heat a bit at their intensity. "Um... I'm not sure."

Jax taps a finger to his chin as he thinks. "It should be wolf themed since ours are related to wolves."

"What do you mean?" I ask.

Luka points to himself as he says, "I'm Apollo, who can often be associated with wolves." He points to Jax. "He's Beta. He was second in command when they worked security for the Underworld." Lastly, he points to Silas. "Alpha. He was the security lead. They were in charge of the Hellhounds."

I nod. "Okay. Well, what name would you like me to have? I don't want to ruin the night by being the only one without a code name. I feel like they are important."

Jax hums thoughtfully before saying, "It wouldn't ruin the night. It's more for your safety. We don't want people to come after you since by coming with us you will now be associated with the Underworld. That's why we have different identities when we associate with them."

I look between all the guys before asking, "So you won't look like this when we go out?"

"No," Luka answers before continuing, "We have altered appearances when we go out in the name of the Underworld. The identities we have now are for the Underground and everyday living. People know we work for the Underworld, but they don't know our association with them.

I tap the fork to my lip. "Okay. So... I need an altered identity when I associate with Persephone versus Jane?"

Silas huffs out a sigh before saying, "Yes. Anyways, back to figuring out a name."

Luka is the first to throw one out. "Arcadia?" It doesn't seem like he likes it though by his pinched brows.

Jax shakes his head. "No. She needs something more goddess-like."

I snort out a laugh. "Goddess-like?"

He grins as he says, "Only the best for you."

I roll my eyes but can't stop the smile from spreading across my face.

"Selene," Silas whispers.

We all looked at Silas, and his eyes widen. He looks just as surprised to have said that out loud. He clears his throat before repeating, "Selene. She's the Goddess of the Moon."

The name seems delicate and soft to me, and I'm surprised Silas is the one who came up with it. Although, by the pink tinge to his cheeks, I'm not the only one surprised by the name. "Selene?"

He turns away from prying eyes and gives a dismissive shrug. "If you don't like it, we can come up with a different one."

Not going to lie, I am enjoying this side of Silas. I smile as I say, "No. No, I like it."

Grunting, he walks around the island toward the elevator and waves a hand in the air. "We should probably go get outfits for the club's theme tonight."

I grin at the two men on either side of me. "Shopping?"

Jax snickers as he kisses the top of my head before walking away. "I'm going to go clean up before we leave."

I laugh as I say, "What? You don't want to smell like post-workout sweat?"

Jax shakes his head with a laugh. "No one but you likes the way I smell after a workout, Mace."

I shrug as he makes his way upstairs. It wasn't a lie. He smells surprisingly delicious after his workouts. I turn to face Luka and ask, "You going to get ready?"

He boops me on the nose and stands from the island. "Sure. Finish your breakfast before you get ready."

I roll my eyes but shove a piece of bacon in my mouth. He ruffles my hair as he walks away. "Good girl."

I feel my cheek heat as I turn back to my food and finish off my breakfast. He makes sure I finish each meal to ensure I stay healthy.

"Why haven't we stopped anywhere for you guys yet?" I ask.

Jax and Luka are on either side of me, each holding one of my hands. The moment we got out of the car, they started fighting over who got to hold my hand. It was humorous until they started pushing each other out of the way to get to me.

I finally told them I had two hands, and they could each take one if they really wanted to hold my hand that badly. Silas had just rolled his eyes and taken the lead.

Jax squeezes my hand softly before answering, "We already have our outfits. This outing is for you. You need a complete outfit."

I arch a brow as I ask, "My outfit includes a crown?"

Luka holds up the bag containing the box with my new crown. "Every goddess needs a crown, does she not?"

I bite my lip as I shrug. I'm not used to anyone buying so much stuff for me, let alone a crown. The crown itself cost at least a few days worth of work. The shop we are heading to for a dress would cost me several weeks' worth of work.

Jax seems to sense my discomfort with accepting gifts, so he lifts my hand to his lips and gives it a soft peck. He smiles down at me as he says, "Let us spoil you."

"But it seems like such a waste of money for you to buy all these things when my stay with you guys is temporary," I whisper.

Luka gives my hand a squeeze as he asks, "Who says it has to be temporary?"

My eyes meet his before shifting to the large man in front of us. Silas continues walking as if he can't hear the conversation going on behind him, but not before I see his body tense.

Although I feel a sharp pain in my chest at what I'm about to say, I say it anyway, "I think temporary is for the best right now. I wouldn't want to impose where I'm not entirely welcome."

Jax and Luka stop walking, jerking me backward as my eyes meet their wide ones. Jax is the first to recover and his eyes narrow on me. "Who says you aren't welcome?"

I huff out a sigh. "No one."

Luka gives my hand a squeeze and asks, "Someone must have made you feel that way for you to say that. Have we somehow made you feel unwelcome?"

I groan as I try to drag them forward. "Forget what I said. Let's catch up with Silas; we are getting behind."

I can tell the two of them want to argue, but at my insistence, they relent. Silas looks over his shoulder, noticing that we are a few paces behind him now. He arches a brow, and I shake my head.

His brows pinch in confusion as he looks between his brothers before landing back on me. "Everything good?"

I nod. "Fine. Let's get to shopping."

He stares for another long moment before nodding. "Okay... let's get this shopping trip over with."

CHAPTER NINETEEN
MACY

Dressed in my outfit for the night, I have to admit, I've never been in anything quite as fancy and beautiful as this. The black bra and skirt alone would be enough for the club, but the sheer black overlay with moons and stars elevates the outfit, making me feel beautiful. My hair is pulled back in a simple, low bun with a few curly strands left loose to frame my face.

My new crown rests proudly on top of my head while I sit on the counter facing Jax. I didn't realize he did make-up until now. His brows are knitted in concentration as he brushes make-up across my upper cheeks.

I jump a bit when he says, "Close your eyes, Sweets."

I do as I'm told and ask, "So, how do you know how to do this?"

He answers a bit distractedly, "I helped a few of the girls at the club Luka used to run years back. I also did Jane's make-up until she got her facial tattoos."

I hum anxiously while I sit with my eyes closed. Then, I shift my hands up so my fingers slip through his belt loops. The brush on my face pauses for a moment before he continues. We sit in comfortable silence until he switches the brush with what I assume is an eyeliner pencil.

I can feel him making stars and dots on my face as he asks softly, "Everything alright, Mace?"

I'm not sure how to answer that. Physically? Yes. Psychologically? Hum... questionable. Emotionally? Now that was the million-dollar question. These men are breaking down my carefully constructed walls, even Silas has a certain hold on me. I know he doesn't want to get close to me, and to be honest, I'm not even sure if he likes me. That doesn't stop me from finding him attractive, though.

I must stay silent for too long because there's a soft squeeze on my thigh as Jax asks, "Macy?"

I huff out a breath and say, "I'm not sure."

Lips meet mine softly before pulling away. I open my eyes, meeting his gentle hazel ones. He's smiling down at me as his eyes flick over my face briefly before meeting mine. "You're beautiful. You know that?"

I can feel the blush heat my cheeks as my eyes shift away from his, slightly embarrassed by the compliment. His thumb brushes across my bottom lip as my eyes meet his again.

His smile turns soft as he says, "With the makeup you look breathtaking. I wish you could see your worth." He lowers so his lips are mere inches from mine and says quietly, "I wish you could see yourself the way I do."

My breath catches as his lips barely brush across mine before he pulls away. "You're ready for the club, Selene."

A shiver shoots down my spine when he calls me my code name. He says it as if he's praying to a goddess. As if I'm meant to be worshiped. "Really?" I ask breathlessly.

His eyes flick over me once more before he nods. "Yes. You want to take a look?"

I shake my head. "No. I trust you."

He smiles as he hands me a mask that was sitting on the counter. "Mind helping me?"

I take it from him with a smirk. "I feel like this is something you can do yourself."

He just shrugs as he lowers to one knee in front of me. "Seems only fitting that the Goddess of the Moon masks her wolf."

I smile and tie the red and silver wolf mask under his bun. It's positioned so it covers the top half of his face and head with the bottom of the mask hovering just over his right eye. A few long blond strands have fallen out of his bun, highlighting his mask perfectly.

He looks up at me from his position on the ground with a soft smile. "Shall we go, my goddess?" He stands gracefully, holding out a hand to help me off the counter.

I slip my hand into his, and he repositions his hold to slip his fingers through mine as we exit my room and head toward the elevator. I hear him chuckle softly to himself as he slips into the elevator.

"What are you chuckling about?"

He gives me a mischievous smile and says, "I'm debating whether or not to get my phone out and take a picture of their faces."

"Their faces?" I ask, slightly confused.

"Luka may fall to his knees and start worshiping at your feet before we even get out the door. Silas won't want to show that he finds you attractive, but I don't think he'll be able to hide behind that stone face of his when he sees you."

I snort as I shake my head. "You're such a shit-stirrer."

He shrugs as the elevator door slides open. "I do love to provoke them."

My laughter fills the room as Jax leads me to the others. Silas and Luka are waiting for us, and they immediately turn when they hear me laughing. I watch in satisfaction as their eyes widen, and their mouths drop.

Jax steps to the side and lifts his arms toward me as if he were awarding a winning prize. I laugh again when he says, "May I present to you, the Goddess of the Moon."

Silas and Luka are both standing there staring at me, seemingly frozen. Did my outfit break them? Silas's dark mohawk is slicked back, and he's wearing a black and gold wolf mask that mirrors Jax's. It seems that for them to become Alpha and Beta, they must wear military cargo pants with a black shirt. My eyes switch to take in Luka, and I notice his eyes are now a warm golden yellow, and his normally brown hair is sprayed with gold paint. He's dressed in a fitted black button-up with gold buttons and black slacks.

Noticing that they are still frozen, I wave my hand in the air. "As flattering as it is to have two wide-eyed males staring at me with their mouths agape, I'm getting a little embarrassed now."

Silas shakes himself, clearing his voice before rubbing the back of his neck. I catch a light tinge of pink on his cheeks before he looks away. "You did good with the make-up, Jax."

Jax grins widely, then meets my gaze as he nods. "I think it's my best work yet."

Silas looks back toward us before heading in our direction. "We should probably head down to the club so we're on time to meet the others."

Jax pecks my cheek with a kiss before following Silas into the elevator. I wait for Luka who claps his hands together as he says, "Yeah. Right. We should head down."

He slips his hand into my waiting one as we step into the elevator. I feel his lips next to my ear as he whispers, "I may be Apollo, but I don't feel worthy enough to gaze upon you. Goddess is too weak a word for your brilliance."

There's a flutter in my stomach as I whisper back, "Thank you."

One of the perks of showing up with the owners of the club is we didn't have to wait in line. The bouncer standing in front of the doors nods toward the guys before pushing the door open for us.

My jaw drops, and I immediately gasp as we enter the large room. All throughout the club there are fake trees, vines, and flowers. There are multiple different stages with dancers dressed up as mythical creatures; fairies, elves, even tanks with mermaids.

Jax bumps my shoulder. "What do you think, Selene?"

Right! I have to remember I'm Selene while I'm here with the Underworld crew. I'm about to answer when a blur suddenly slams into me. Thankfully, Luka and Jax catch the blur and I before we fall to the ground.

I let out a choked laugh when I see Jane pull away with a wide grin.

Silas growls. "Seph! We just arrived. You could have let Selene settle in before you attacked."

I grin as she pulls me away from Jax and drags me in the direction of the dance floor. Over her shoulder, she yells, "She's mine now, fuckers!"

I can't stop giggling as she turns around to face me and begins moving to the beat in the middle of the dance floor. I smile as I say, "I didn't realize you wanted to dance with me so badly, Persephone."

"It's Seph to you, bitch!" She laughs as she rubs up next to me. Waggling her brows at me, she asks, "Selene?"

I roll my eyes. "The guys came up with it." I look around and notice that two of her men are next to us. Both of them give me a smirk and a wink.

Yelling so that she can be heard over the music, she says, "Goddess of the Moon. Seems fitting."

I point to her two guys next to us as I say, "Seems you have two guardians on the dance floor."

With a look over her shoulder, she smiles, then turns back to me with a laugh. "Those boys wouldn't let me come out here unless I had protection. It works out though, because Charon and Cerberus love to dance."

I move a bit closer to her so I can quietly speak into her ear. I play it off as dancing while we grind up against each other. "How's the pregnancy going?"

She groans. "Morning sickness is a bitch and a half."

I snort. "The magic of pregnancy I've heard."

"Magic my ass," she huffs out.

Suddenly, we are jerked out of our conversation by a man bumping into us. We both turn toward him, letting out a sigh when it's obvious that he's drunk.

I notice Alec and Howe don't move from their positions, but they do have an eye on the situation.

The man's sour breath hits my nostrils as he says, "Wow, sorry." He hiccups before his eyes widen on us. "Wow, you're fucking hot! Did it hurt when you fell from heaven?"

Seph and I look at each other before she bursts out in laughter. She looks down at her nails before giving the male a creepy as fuck grin. "No, darling. But I did break a few nails when I crawled up from the Underworld."

I snicker as I add, "But your nails are so flawless."

She laughs as she teases, "Oh, I know. I had them replaced with claws."

The drunk man looks utterly confused by our banter but doesn't seem to get the memo to back off as he takes a step closer. As if choreographed, Seph pulls the feather out of her hair at the same time as I pull out my knife that's hidden under my skirt. The slits in the overlay provide perfect access to them in a pinch.

Seph's knife meets his neck while mine rests on his precious cock. The music stopped at some point and the club is utterly silent, I now notice. I can hear growling and laughing, but with my focus on the man in front of us, I'm not sure who it is.

Seph's voice is deadly when she says, "You obviously don't know who I am, so let me introduce myself. My name is Persephone, Queen of the Underworld."

As soon as the title passes her lips, the haze instantly clears from the man's eyes. Seems he sobered up real quick. His eyes widen and he sputters, "I'm so sorry! I'm so sorry! I didn't mean nothin by it."

She presses the knife harder against his neck. "Men like you never do until they're caught."

He whimpers, and I watch as his eyes start to water. Looking down, I find a sudden wet spot where my knife is. "Fuck!" I growl in disgust as I pull my knife away. "You fucking pissed on my knife, dude!"

"I'm sorry! I'm sorry," he whimpers.

Seph rolls her eyes as she pulls her knife away from his neck. "Fucking pathetic. Run along."

He doesn't need to be told twice. In his haste to escape, he trips over himself, nearly knocking people over as he goes. Booming laughter suddenly fills the room from multiple directions. In front of me, Howe and Alec are holding onto each other while wiping their eyes from laughing so hard.

I look over my shoulder to find Jax slapping his knee in laughter. Luka is standing beside him shaking his head as he snickers. Silas is the first to break the silence as he growls out, "Where the fuck did she get a knife?"

I point toward Jax with the tip of my knife before sheathing it back into the thigh holster. I can hear Seph giggling behind me, so I look back to see what she finds so funny, but she's looking at the opposite corner of the room.

Following her line of sight, I find her other two males, Jace and Zane. I'm not sure what she's laughing about until I notice both of them are covering the front of their pants.

I hear Seph say quietly, "They get turned on when I use my knives."

I smirk as I tease, "So can we still dance, or are they going to run over here and throw you over their shoulder like cavemen?"

She shakes her head as she turns back to me. "Nope. Tonight is my last night to have fun before I get fat. That means you have to drink for me too."

The music starts back up, and I laugh as I begin to dance again. "I didn't realize I was drinking for you tonight."

She puts her hands together in a prayer motion as she sticks out her lower lip. "Please, oh please, do this for me, Selene! It's what best friends do!"

I roll my eyes as I snicker. "Fine. But I didn't see that in the best friends handbook."

She arches a brow. "There's a handbook?"

I shrug. "Fuck if I know."

She laughs and yells over her shoulder to the guys, "Get this girl a shot! She's drinking for both of us tonight!"

Both guys look to me for confirmation, and I nod. Howe nods and makes his way over to the bar.

"Drinking tonight, Selene?" Luka whispers into my ear, causing me to jump. When did he get behind me?

With a smile, I say, "Apparently, it's what best friends do."

His laugh is light as he questions, "Best friends?"

Seph nods as she replies, "Of course! She's the only one with a uterus around here. I'm constantly surrounded by testosterone. Every once in a while, I need some estrogen."

Luka laughs as Alec comes up behind Seph and says, "You love our testosterone."

Her tone is playful as she retorts, "I didn't say I didn't love it. I need some variety in my life, though."

Howe interrupts, holding out two shots in my direction. "One for you and one for Seph."

I take the one for me and quickly shoot it back, shivering as it burns its way down. My voice is hoarse as I ask, "What the fuck was that?"

He grins. "Hell's Belly. It's fireball whiskey and some other stuff. I didn't exactly listen to what the bartender said was in it."

Clearing my throat, I reach for the next one. It's a pretty blue with what looks like glitter floating in it. I shoot it back fast, not trusting Howe's taste in alcohol.

I lick my lips after, not hating that one. Handing the glass back to him, I ask, "What was that one?"

"Glitter Bomb."

It takes a few moments, but I can feel the alcohol dulling my senses as I dance. I enjoy the feeling of being between Seph and Luka as I feel the pulse of the beat around me. Fuck, I love dancing.

It feels like it's been hours when I hear Luka's soft voice, "It's time to go home, babe."

I whine as I continue to dance, "I don't want to yet."

His laugh is soft as he says, "I know. But the club is about to close. It's time to go home."

My body slows as his words sink in. "Home?"

Suddenly, his hazel eyes appear in front of me, and he cups my cheeks with his hands as he says, "Yeah, home."

Feeling sluggish all of a sudden, I let out a hum of acknowledgement. The dancing and alcohol must be catching up to me. "Yeah... home..." I mumble.

His smile is gentle as he nods. For a moment, he lowers down, then I'm lifted into the air. I let out a squeak of surprise. He kisses my forehead as he begins to walk. "I got you."

I snuggle closer into his chest, letting his warmth seep into me. I feel tired now and let my eyes slowly close as I'm lulled to sleep by his heartbeat. I feel so safe in his arms.

Silas

I huff out a sigh as we enter the house. Well, that plan went to shit. I spent the entire time watching my brothers, and their eyes never once drifted from Macy.

Suddenly, a drunk, half-asleep girl is placed in my arms. I look up to find Luka with a shit-eating grin on his face as he walks away. "Help her up to her room, won't you, brother?"

My eyes narrow at his retreating form. I look over to find a snickering Jax. "What?" I growl out.

He shakes his head as he moves quickly toward the stairs. "Nothing. Have a good night!"

I watch as my two younger brothers abandon me with the very girl I am trying to get them to forget. Shaking my head, I head to the elevator.

Macy stirs in my arms when the elevator begins to move. She looks up at me with hazy eyes. "Silas?"

"Yes."

She seems a bit confused for a moment before she hums. Her eyes are still on me as the elevator door opens. I head down the hallway as she asks, "Do you not like me?"

I'm caught off guard by the sudden question, but thankfully not enough to show it on my face. I huff out a sigh, irritated that my brothers put me in this situation.

"No," I say sternly as I try to readjust her in my arms so I can open the door to her room. It's dark inside as the door swings open.

Making my way over to her bed, I gently set her down. With sleepy eyes, she looks up at me and asks, "So you do like me?"

I'm not sure how to answer that question. It would reveal too much if I answered honestly. I don't want this girl to know all my secrets, even if she is drunk. She probably won't remember this conversation anyways.

"Do you hate me?" she whispers. Her voice sounds sad as she asks that. Why would she care if I liked or hated her anyway? She has my brothers under her spell. Why do I matter?

My hands are still on her bare foot, her heels now sitting at the edge of the bed. Her eyes are still watching me. Those fucking beautiful hazel-green eyes. Eyes that see too much of me for my liking. I should say yes. Yes, I hate her. That's all I need to say, and it would make every encounter after this so much easier.

But with her soft gaze on mine, I can't lie. Huffing out a breath, I say, "No."

Releasing her foot, I set her shoes on the ground. She snuggles into the bed a bit, then shivers. Biting my lip, I pull the covers up and over her. I should leave now. I got her to her room.

Hovering at the edge of her bed beside her, I watch as her breaths slow and her body relaxes. I reach forward without thought, my fingers brushing softly over her cheek as I move a stray lock of hair back behind her ear.

She doesn't wake so I huff a sigh into the darkness. "I hate what you are doing to me," I whisper, "I was content. I didn't mind the cage that held me or the beast that controlled my every move. The cage and beast were of my own making. They kept me content."

Lost to the moment, I bend down and press a soft kiss to her forehead before turning to leave. "You make me wish for more. Yearn for something I shouldn't."

I pause at the door and look over my shoulder, taking in her sleeping form. She looks so peaceful. I wish I could find that kind of peace. My fingers tighten on the doorframe as I rip my gaze away. "I'm sorry," I whisper, "I know I'm going to hurt you."

I walk out the door without looking back. Biting the inside of my cheek, I work on fortifying my walls. I can barely feel my fingers due to how tightly clenched my fists are. Once the elevator door closes, I thump my forehead against the cool metal. "You can do this," I whisper, "This is for your brothers. This is for you."

With one last thump of my head against the metal, I let my body soak in the cool touch. I back away, looking at my reflection. I can see the change in my features but most of all my eyes. The man looking back at me is the wolf I had to become, the beast heartless and cold.

I nod once at my reflection. "I am a beast of my own making." Logic is what I need. Hearts are for those who can afford to lose them. I lost mine the day my brother was murdered, and that's how it needs to stay.

CHAPTER TWENTY
SILAS

Five months. It's been five long months since Macy started living with us. Five months where I've had to watch as she has beguiled my brothers. If she thinks she will be able to lead me around by my dick like she does them, she's wrong. I won't make that mistake. My older brother made that mistake, and where did it leave him? A hole between the eyes and buried six feet down. Betrayed by the woman he loved. And I'll be here when Macy does the same to my brothers. I'll be here to protect them and pick up the shattered pieces.

But... if I'm being honest, she isn't actually leading them by their dicks. They are doing this because they want to. I can see it in their soft gazes and genuine smiles. I can tell that their dicks aren't the only things involved. Their hearts are involved too.

That doesn't stop the irritation I feel when I see my brothers with her, though, and if I'm truthful, I want a relationship with her too. I need her to look at me the way she looks at them. I crave her soft touch. I hunger to bathe in her moonlit smiles. The beast in me wants that comfort more than I am willing to admit.

As the days pass, I am slowly becoming more beast than man. My dark side consuming me more and more each day. I don't want to feel. I don't want to hunger for her. If I let my beast control my every move, that means I no longer have to be human. If I'm no longer human, I no longer have a heart to break.

The shrill ringing of my phone has me looking down to find Marvin's name flash across the screen. I growl in frustration before answering. "What?"

"Hello, sir. How is my escort treating you?"

"Fine. Why?" I know he wants something, otherwise he wouldn't be calling.

"The cash you have been paying is more than adequate for her services. But I would like for her to be back under my control."

"Why do you need her back?"

His hesitation makes me sit up at attention. "Well, sir... she's been under my care for so long, and I only wish for her to come home."

I snort out a derisive laugh. "I doubt that. Spit out what you want before I hang up."

"I'll trade you for her back."

"What could you possibly have that I would want?"

There's an air of satisfaction in his voice as he replies, "The location of your brother's murderer."

I'm shocked into silence for a long moment before asking, "How could you possibly know where he is?"

"I've had my girls out looking. One of them came back with his name and location. So do we have a deal?"

"A deal?" I growl out in question.

"My escort for the location or your brother's killer?"

My heart beats fast as a war erupts within me. Before I can think too much about it I say, "Yes."

I can hear his smile through the phone as he says, "Good. How about tomorrow evening?"

"Fine." I hang up without letting him get another word in. I can feel the pounding of my heartbeat in my head as I try to control my breathing over what I've just agreed to. I take a deep breath in and hold it until I feel the burn in my chest. As I slowly blow out the breath, I slam my emotions down deep inside me, fortifying the stone wall around my heart. Just like I had before I met Macy.

I can feel my mask sliding back into place as I let my dark side take over. I know my brothers are going to hate me for this, but it doesn't matter. We are finally going to get revenge on the man who killed our brother. That is more important than any woman. Steeling myself, I let the next thought consume me.

Revenge is more important than a whore for hire.

Macy

What the fuck am I doing? I never thought I would be at this house longer than a few weeks, let alone five months. Five months since the Steepe brothers came and picked me up at my apartment saying that I was theirs.

I'm surprised Marvin hasn't asked for me back considering I'm his highest-paid escort. The money the brothers are paying him for my company must be enough to keep him off my ass. My phone hasn't rung with his name on the caller ID in weeks. I've been holding my breath, hoping I don't. Figuratively, not literally.

Each day I wake up in my bed, I'm expecting this to have been a dream, or for Silas to come in saying that my time with them is over. That I have to return to Marvin and my sad excuse of a life.

My heart thumps wildly at the thought, and I have to bite my lip to stop the sudden burn behind my eyes. I know I will eventually have to return to my real life; this is only a temporary arrangement. But the thought of leaving them now hurts more than I wanted to admit.

Fuck, I let these men rip apart my walls with their claws. These three wolves who have a bond like no other. A pack where I don't belong. That doesn't stop me from yearning to be the moon they howl at, though. To be worshiped and gazed upon with something other than lust and hunger.

At this moment, I've never been more thankful to be alone. The tears slide down my cheeks as I stare up at the ceiling. Selene. I've never wanted to be someone else more than I do at this moment. I want to be Selene instead of Macy more than my next breath.

Selene would be able to keep the three wolves. She would be able to stay and call them hers forever. I cover my mouth as a sob slips through. Jumping up from the bed, I rush into the bathroom, locking the door behind me.

I quickly strip and turn the shower on with fumbling hands. My vision blurs as I stand under the warm spray, letting the water pour over me. I let myself break for just this moment as I slide down the wall. Sitting on the floor of the shower, I sob into my hand as my heart shreds into thousands of pieces. I will never be Selene.

I will forever be Macy. The moment it's time to leave, I won't be Mace or Mac anymore. Just Macy. Fucking Macy! I've never hated being myself more than in this moment because I know it will eventually come to an end.

I'm ripped out of my self-inflicted pity party by a knock on my door. Taking a few deep breaths, I answer, "Yes?"

Luka's soft voice greets me in reply. "Sorry, Mac. I knocked on your bedroom door, and there was no answer. I heard the shower going and came in. I didn't mean to invade your privacy."

I give a watery chuckle as a few more tears slip free. Always the considerate one. "It's fine, Luka. What's up?"

He clears his throat before saying, "Didn't mean to interrupt your personal time, but I wanted to let you know Silas called a meeting with me and Jax. We will be in the office in the club downstairs."

I nod before realizing he can't see me. "That's okay. Take your time."

He taps the door again as he says, "Lunch is downstairs. Make sure you eat, Mac."

My head thumps against the wall as I try not to let anymore sobs slip through. I take a deep breath before replying, "Will do." I wait for the door to my bedroom to close before I let the sobs out. I am going to miss this, and I haven't even left yet.

Luka's constant badgering to make sure I'm eating because I forget otherwise. I will miss laughing hysterically at Jax attacking me with hugs and kisses when he's all sweaty after his workouts. Hell, I will even miss Silas's dark eyes tracking my every move as if he were a predator stalking his prey.

I know the moment I walk away from them my world will lose its luster, its shine. Colors will turn dark and depressing. Warmth will turn frigid at being alone yet again. All alone. Again.

CHAPTER TWENTY-ONE
SILAS

I sent my brothers a text about ten minutes ago telling them we needed to talk. Now, I'm waiting for them in the office. I knew it would take them a bit considering I told them to meet me in the office at the club. I don't want Macy accidentally overhearing our discussion. Especially if it goes the way I think it will.

I don't need my brother's running to her right after I tell them what I decided. I am the leader of this family, no matter how much I don't want to be. This position wasn't supposed to be mine. It was supposed to be Grayson's role, and I was to be his second-in-command.

That thought alone hardens my resolve. This is what needs to be done. My body stiffens the moment I hear a knock at the door. Here we go. "Come in."

Jax enters first with his normal smile and swagger. No. Not his normal smile. His smile has become more genuine since meeting Macy. He nods as he slumps into the chair in front of my desk.

Luka follows in behind, closing the door to silence the pulsing music of the club. It may be lunch time, but the employees like to plan the playlist for the night. Which means constant music and dancing.

When he turns, I notice he has a frown, and his brows are furrowed. I arch a brow when his eyes finally meet mine. He shakes his head as he says, "Don't worry about it. I'll figure it out."

I tend to not argue with my youngest brother, but this seems more personal than work related. "Sure?"

He nods. "Yeah. Something seemed off with Macy, but I'm sure it's nothing."

Well shit. That isn't going to help with the current conversation. Best to start off slow before ripping the band-aid off. If I start too soon, he'll run back up to her. Clearing my throat, I start with work. "Very well. I want an update on everything you two are working on. We haven't talked business much since Macy came to live with us."

Jax shrugs as he answers, "No update on my end. We have managed the problem of the illegal skin trade. The local gangs know who runs this area as well as who owns the Underground. We haven't seen much pushback." He runs his fingers through his long hair. "The ladies in the district haven't reported any issues with Johns or Janes causing problems for them. Also, the pimps seem to be abiding by the rules."

I nod but inwardly cringe. I forgot Jax was in charge of the escorts and prostitutes. He will still have access to Macy after this deal. Fucking hell. I've managed to complicate my life over this fucking woman.

I look to Luka and ask, "And on your end?"

He shrugs. "We haven't had any issues with harder drugs finding their way into the clubs. I think the show of power we did a few years ago sent a firm message on our views of certain drugs."

I nod. "Good. Good."

"Get on with it, brother," Jax says with a smirk. "We all know you didn't call us down here for an update on work. You could have done that in your office upstairs. You specifically wanted to make sure Mace couldn't hear whatever you have to say."

My eyes narrow. "Always so observant brother."

He shrugs. "Need to be. You taught me that."

I huff out a sigh. He does have a point. "I got a call from Marvin."

They both look at me with wide eyes before Jax snorts out a laugh. "What did that fucker want?"

"He had info he wanted to sell us."

Luka looks confused as he asks, "What information does he think he can sell us? We know everything that goes on in this city. Even have eyes and ears in the surrounding territories."

My fingers begin tapping the top of the desk as I say, "He has information on a certain person he thought we would be interested in."

Jax shakes his head with a laugh. "Who does he think we would be interested in?"

My eyes meet theirs before falling to the desk. "The man who killed our brother."

The room is completely silent before Jax barks out a laugh. "Seriously? We have been looking for that man for years. What makes him think he has found what we haven't been able to?"

"He has a few girls that go to the man's house regularly. Apparently, one of his girls overheard him blustering about killing one of the famous Steepe brothers."

Luka's eyes narrow. "He wouldn't give us that information for free, Si. What does he want?"

Jax snorts. "It isn't fucking true. We've had eyes and ears all over this city. There's no way one of his girls found the man we've spent years looking for."

I keep my eyes cast downward as I say, "I've confirmed the information with the girl to make sure he wasn't blowing smoke up our ass. What his girl says is true."

"What does he want, Silas?" Luka repeats with a growl.

I don't understand why I'm suddenly losing my nerve. My eyes lift to meet Luka's, and I'm met with cold hazel eyes. He knows. He knows what I'm about to say. "The only thing he's ever wanted."

Luka jerks from his seat as he leans onto the desk. His eyes are ice cold, and his jaw tightens before his voice comes out dark and emotionless. He punctuates each word as he asks, "What. Did. He. Ask. For?"

I look up at him, matching his emotionless tone as I reply, "You know what he asked for."

"Then say it. Shouldn't be that hard if you feel absolutely nothing," he challenges.

I pause for a moment, smashing down the pang I feel in my chest. No. There's no place for that right now. "He wants her."

Jax finally speaks up. "Her? You don't mean…"

Luka interrupts him, "That's exactly what he means."

Jax rises from his chair as well. I turn to look at him, and the look on his face is one I've never seen on him before. Let alone directed at me. Horror. Utter horror at what I could have possibly done. "You told him to fuck off, right?"

When I don't respond, I watch the horror grow. He shakes his head in denial. "You told him… you told him to fuck off, Silas?"

My jaw tightens as I switch my gaze back to Luka. I can see the shimmer in his eyes. Glassy with the emotions I'm sure are bubbling over within him. His voice is gruff as he says, "Please… please tell me you didn't."

I'm relying on the cold and heartless beast within me as I say in a dead voice, "I am the leader of this family. I will do what's best for us. If turning over a whore is how we get the information we need for revenge, then there's no question of what to do next."

Luka grabs random papers off my desk and throws them across the room. "Fuck you, Silas! Fuck you! We are a family! We make decisions together!"

Trying to ignore his outburst, I continue, "We will be handing her over tomorrow morning. Once he receives her he will give us the information about the man who killed our brother."

Jax shakes his head as he kicks the chair across the room. "You are not handing Mace over to that fucker."

"I will do what is necessary to protect our family. You two have gotten too invested in a woman who is temporary. She was not meant to be a permanent resident in our lives."

"You may feel that way but not us," Jax growls.

"You are my priority, not her. She will betray us just like all the others. She was only ever here to be a temporary plaything, nothing but a whore." My face explodes with pain. I don't raise a hand to my jaw as I turn to face Jax.

His arm is still extended from punching me, his breathing is coming out in huffs, and his eyes shimmer with rage. "Don't you EVER call her that again."

I spit out a glob of blood. My eyes meet his with unwavering conviction. "It does not change anything. Hit me all you want, but the decision has been made. She will be handed over tomorrow for the information. I would advise you to distance yourself for the night to make the transition easier."

Jax shakes his head as he walks away. "You're a right fucking bastard."

I shrug. "I've been called worse, brother."

"Fuck off." He opens the door, walking out and slamming it behind him.

My eyes shift to Luka. "Anything you would like to say, brother. Would you like to get in a shot?"

He shakes his head with a humorless laugh. He turns walking away. "Wouldn't it hurt more if I didn't? Physical pain eventually recedes, but you deserve for it to linger."

"Luka, this is for the best."

He pauses at the door, before looking over his shoulder. My chest tightens at the pain on his face. Tears slide down his cheeks as he asks, "Better for who? You or her?"

"Luka," I say gruffly.

He shakes his head. "Don't. I'll follow along with your plan. I know my place in this family. But just know you've lost Jax and I. We are done. From now on, I'll just be like all of your other employees."

"Luka!"

He turns, opening the door but pausing to say, "I have always loved and respected you, but I won't forgive you for this." He walks out, closing the door softly behind him.

The softness of that door closing hurts more than when Jax slammed it. Huffing out a sigh, my head falls to the desk. I bang it a few times trying to get the pain in my head to override the boulder sitting on my chest.

My brothers have always meant more to me than anything else in this world. Right now, I feel like they're just as lost to me as Grayson. "Grayson," my voice breaks on his name. "What would you do? You were the leader not me. It was never supposed to be me."

I squeeze my eyes shut. "I need your help, brother. What do I do?" I'm greeted only by silence. My eyes burn as I say, "Yeah...Yeah that's what I thought. You've abandoned me too."

CHAPTER TWENTY-TWO
SILAS

Seeing Marvin's disgusting smile has me second guessing myself. Was Macy really worth the knowledge? Maybe we could have found the information a different way. I hold her upper arm as I stare at Marvin. The man makes me sick. I can see the gleam in his eyes when he looks at her. We haven't had issues with him. He always treats his female escorts and prostitutes the way we require. But I have a weird feeling that Macy is different for him.

"I see you decided to take my deal," Marvin says with a snicker. "I knew you wouldn't be able to refuse."

I look down at Macy to find her eyes wild as she looks around trying to figure out what's going on. I look back up at Mavin with a sneer. "I told you, I would take the deal. I am a man of my word." My eyes shift back to Macy when I hear her panicked breathing.

I can see the hysteria building as she looks up at me. "What... what's going on?"

Marvin laughs gleefully as he says, "Didn't you know, girl? You are being traded for information."

She looks back up at me with wide eyes. "Please... please don't do this. I'll do anything! Please don't give me back to him," she begs.

I feel a burn begin in my chest. But I ignore it and her. I need to do this. I need this for my family. Jax and Luka don't like this plan. They flat out refused to talk to me this morning when we were heading here. I saw the side looks from Luka. The plea in his eyes for me not to do this, but I ignored them. We don't need a woman. We need justice for Grayson. This is more important. Without letting myself think too much about it, I throw her at the pimp. "There. You have your whore back. Give me what I'm owed."

Marvin smirks down at her as he grabs her arm. "Thought you could get away from me, did you?"

She's not looking at him. Her eyes are still on me, pleading. "Please."

I ignore the words. I ignore the spear of pain in my chest. I've had to ignore my feelings ever since Grayson died. I've had to bury every emotion. So I do what I'm good at and mask. Forcing a sneer on my face I say, "You're nothing more than a street whore." I can feel my brothers stiffen behind me, but they don't show their distaste for my words. They wouldn't dare. But I can feel their eyes boring into the back of my head.

She jerks as if I've slapped her. I watch as the light in her eyes dims, and she stops fighting. I immediately want to take the words back, but I don't. I need this information. I need her to hate us so she never comes back.

Marvin looks at me and smiles. "The man you're looking for lives on Dixon Street. It's the purple house, and you can't miss it. Has boards covering the windows." He nods to us and turns, dragging Macy behind him. She doesn't fight. The woman we met seems to have disappeared. The wolf cub is gone. Our shining moon. Gone. She looks back at us briefly, and I see it. She's lost hope. I... I broke her.

I fucking broke her, but it's too late to fix it now. I got what I needed, and I can finally carry out the revenge we've been seeking for the last several years. A whore's life isn't worth more than the death of the man who killed my brother. Right?

Then why does the thought of calling her a whore again taste like rotten meat? I watch as she's dragged away from us... from me. The only thing I can think right now is how I want to rush over there and rip her out of his grasp. I'm not thinking of my brother... I'm thinking of her.

Shaking myself, I force my body to turn. I catch the looks in my brothers' eyes before I shake those off too and continue walking toward my car. Their eyes are empty now. Seems I broke them as well. Shouldn't be a surprise. I'm great at breaking things.

My voice is rough as I yell out, "Get in the fucking car. We have places to be."

It takes a moment before they turn and head to the car. They both slide in quietly, refusing to talk to me. Doesn't surprise me, and I'm fine with it. The car roars to life, and out of the corner of my eye, I watch Jax pull out a carton of smokes.

I feel a tightening in my chest as I look over to find him peering down at the carton for a moment before ripping the plastic off. It takes him a few minutes, but he manages to find a lighter.

Placing the cig between his lips, he takes a deep inhale. He coughs for a moment before taking another. I look away. He's been smoke free for over six months. Not a single cigarette that whole time. All because of her. He did it for her.

I'm white knuckling the steering wheel as we make our way to the address Marvin gave me. Killing this man will fix everything. It will. I can feel my beast; he wants to take over. His need for bloodshed and revenge. I don't even hesitate. Feeling the void of nothingness when I let myself go is better than the deep-seated ache I feel in my chest right now.

Macy

I'm done. I finally trusted someone. No scratch that, multiple someone's, and they turned on me. Just like all the others. There's a deep-seated pain in my chest that pulses with each beat of my heart. What's the point in living in this world if everyone is going to betray me? I can't live like this anymore. I had a taste of freedom. I finally got away from Marvin, and they handed me right back. They handed me back like I meant nothing to them. Absolutely nothing.

They called me their moon goddess, but I was only a wolf pup. A wolf pup trying to find a pack. They removed my leash for six glorious months and then leashed me again without a second of hesitation. Handed my leash back to Marvin like a dog. I belong to Marvin. Again.

He throws me down on the bed roughly. I look up to find him smirking. "You can stay here and think about what you've done."

Think about what I've done? What I've done is trust people I clearly shouldn't have. I trusted in general, and I knew from the very beginning that I shouldn't have. I fell for their charm. Huffing out a sigh as I look up at my captor, I don't fight. Why should I? Fighting has only ever led me to end up in his grasp once more. I fought like they told me, only to end up back here. I lie on the bed unmoving.

His smirk widens as he says, "Seems those guys broke you finally. Maybe you will be a good little doll now."

I stare up at him, not moving, frozen in my attempt to become numb. I hear a zipper and look over to find him pulling down his pants. In the past, I would have screamed and fought because I know what he wants. He wants to fuck me. Wants to own me. I've never let him. I would never have let this disgusting man touch me before. But now? Now... I'm tired. I'm bone tired of fighting. I just want to be numb. Being numb is better than feeling the utter agony of my heart-shattering.

I'm motionless when he rips off my pants. He slithers up the bed until he's hovering over me. He slides my underwear to the side and presses his cock to my entrance.

There's a little voice in my head yelling at me to push him away. Fight. Scream. Anything to get him off me. But the numbness has finally taken over. That little voice cannot help to control my mind as I am now. My mind is gone. My heart shattered. His whiskey and weed scent engulfs me. The urge to recoil in disgust is there, but my body stays frozen. He slams his cock into me. My mind screams in pain, but my voice is gone. I'm paralyzed within my own mind.

"God, you're so tight! I've wanted to fuck this cunt for so long." He continues slamming into me, over and over, grunting with each thrust. I can feel tears sliding down my cheeks and into my hair as my mind tries to rebel against what's happening. My vision begins to blur and the urge to sob gets stuck in the back of my throat. My heart and mind are in a battle of wills.

"Cry for me, baby. That's it. Take my fucking cock like a good little whore." He grunts as he smirks down at me. He slams into me hard one last time, and I feel his hot come fill me. He's panting hard above me. He smacks a sloppy wet kiss against my lips as he pulls away. "So good now that you're broken."

He pulls out of me. I can feel his come leaking out and onto the sheets. "Be a good girl and stay," he orders as he tucks his come-soaked dick back into his pants. He runs a hand through his hair and starts to laugh. "Your cunt is as good as the clients say. I think I'll keep you for a while as my personal toy."

I lie on the bed, staring up at the brown-stained ceiling. I want to tell him to fuck off. The need to scrub every inch of my skin to get him off me is strong. The compulsion to scrub my skin till it bleeds, but I can't move. I think about his words before succumbing to darkness' embrace. I stay like a good girl. I do. Because... I'm done.

His booming laugh fills the room, and the last words I hear before I'm completely consumed are, "I knew I could break you."

CHAPTER TWENTY-THREE
SILAS

It's been a few weeks since I handed Macy back over to Marvin. Fucking three weeks to be exact. And my brothers haven't spoken to me since that day. Not a single word. Neither of them have acknowledged my presence once. They haven't even looked at me. It's as if I'm a ghost inside my own house. Which frankly is pissing me off. Why the fuck am I a ghost in my own home?

Jax seems pissed all the time, and is constantly smoking. I haven't seen him without a cig in his mouth the last three weeks. He's either on the balcony smoking or in the gym punching the shit out of the bags. I've had to replace three already. Which is a feat in itself. I make sure to buy heavy-duty punching bags due to how much wear the damn things go through. I've seen his bloody knuckles when he comes back upstairs.

Thinking about my youngest brother has me huffing out an irritated sigh. He's been completely silent. Hardly eats, and if he does eat, it's the snacks Macy used to eat. I've noticed that Luka has been staying in the room we let Macy use instead of his own. The stupid room that was supposed to be a guest room but was taken over with all of her stuff. I think I broke him the moment I broke Macy.

I look up from my cup of coffee to find Jax leaning against the frame of the balcony door. He's staring blankly out at the city lights around us. He's smoking his last cigarette, so I know he's going to leave soon. I hear shuffling behind me, so I look over my shoulder to find Luka walking away from the stairs with the custom Squishmallow he bought Macy. It's the noodle. Stupid fucking thing if you ask me. I remember Luka buying it because he was jealous of the nickname Jax had given her. He told me he was going to start calling her Mac. I've never seen my brother blush as hard as he did when he told me that.

She was his little macaroni, and he was her cheese. At least, that's what he said. Again, I thought it was stupid, and Jax had laughed for hours when he heard him say it. But Macy, she thought it was the sweetest nickname ever. I watch as he clutches it tightly to his chest and flops onto the couch.

Anger builds within my chest, replacing the hollow ache that has been there for the last week. The weeks before, all I could feel was the deep abyss of numbness after avenging the murder of my brother. My eyes meet the black abyss of my coffee, and my muscles coil as my anger grows into a strengthening storm. My grip on the mug tightens as I feel my arm raise up and throw it at the wall in front of me. The ceramic shattering echoes around us as I watch the dark liquid run down the wall like blood. My vision blurs as I remember the blood splattering everything around me when I killed the man who murdered my brother.

I shake myself out of the memory as I slam my fist onto the counter. Fuck this! My family is fucking falling apart over a woman! Why the fuck are they acting like this? Our family broke once because a woman betrayed us causing our brother to be killed! The eyes of my brothers finally meet mine for the first time in weeks. My breaths come quick as I sneer at them, "Why the fuck are you both acting like she meant something? She was a temporary woman. Temporary! She wasn't meant to stay here forever! Yeah, she was fun, but we killed the man who killed Grayson. She was a means to an end. Why aren't you celebrating?!"

Jax rolls his eyes as he responds, "I haven't seen you celebrating either, brother."

It feels as if a cold bucket of water douses my fiery anger. Frozen at the accusation. He's right, I haven't. I blacked out the moment we stormed into that man's house. I remember having a knife in my hand. I was satisfied for only a few moments after I felt the blood on my hands, but... that's it. Only a few moments of satisfaction and then my stomach turned to lead. I don't remember much after that. The next thing I knew, I was waking up in my bed. No longer covered in blood.

Jax huffs out a dark laugh. "You have been moping around this house just as much as we have."

I growl as I yell, "No, I have not! She meant nothing!" The moment those words leave my mouth I feel a stabbing pain where my cold, dead heart remains. Her face flashes through my mind. The look of utter betrayal that passed across her features. I remember the light leaving her eyes as she accepted the truth.

"How's that lie working out for you?" Luka speaks up from the couch.

I slam a fist on the island again, not allowing myself to react to the shot of pain stabbing through my hand. Fuck! Her face is seared into my brain. Her smiling face turned to a twisted sort of frown because of what I did. "Fuck this!" I yell as I turn to head toward the elevator.

"Where are you going?" Jax yells from behind me.

Pressing the button, I yell back over my shoulder, "To get our wolf cub."

She was more than our wolf cub, but I don't deserve to call her our moon goddess. Even if she was. I hear the pounding of hurried footsteps heading toward me as I walk into the elevator. I turn to find them entering behind me without hesitation.

Jax inhales a lungful of smoke before stubbing his cigarette out on the bottom of his shoe. He manages to throw it into the trash before the doors close. His smirk is mocking as he lets the smoke seep out of his nostrils. "What makes you think she will want to come back here after what we did?"

Still facing forward, I answer, "She won't have a choice."

Luka speaks up from my other side. "Shouldn't she have one? Considering the shit you said to her."

I shrug, not really giving a fuck. I need to fix my family. My heart may want to apologize for what I said and did, but I have NEVER apologized for doing what was best for my family. Not once have I apologized for my actions as the head of this family; I'm not about to start now. Although, if her face keeps haunting me like it is, that may have to change.

CHAPTER TWENTY-FOUR
MACY

I don't know how long it's been. Maybe a few weeks. The only time I see Marvin is when he comes in to fuck me, and I only get out of bed to use the bathroom. He wipes me down after he fucks me and then he leaves. He does force water down my throat, and I eat a few crackers when he won't leave unless I eat.

I hear a loud bang downstairs, but I ignore it. Probably just a druggie or one of the girls. I continue staring at the wall but jump when my door slams open.

"Macy?" I stiffen at the voice. No. No... he wouldn't.

Then another voice says, "Mace?" No, not him too! Please. Please tell me not all three of them are here.

My question is answered when a voice calls, "Mac? Macaroni?" No! I bury my head under the pillow.

"Fuck! Macy." I hear Silas' voice from the doorway.

I feel the bed dip beside me, and a hand touches my shoulder lightly. I jerk away from the touch. "What the fuck do you want? Leave me the hell alone!" I've felt so empty the last few weeks but now? Now, all I feel is anger. How dare they show up here!

Silas sighs and says, "I'm... We're here to rescue you."

I've never heard him sound so defeated, but I don't care. I sit up in bed. Slightly dizzy from the movement, I steady myself before glaring at him.

"Why the fuck would I need rescuing?" I look at the two brothers behind him. "You two didn't do a damn thing," I screech as I point at Silas, but my eyes are still on Jax and Luka. "When he handed me over."

They all look away, including Silas. Silas sighs and says, "I'm sorry."

Normally his apology would throw me off, but right now, I'm filled with too much rage. I scoff. "Sorry? You're sorry?!"

Jax speaks up from the corner, "We are sorry. We shouldn't have handed you over. No matter what."

I let out a humorless laugh. "Yeah... well. I hope the information was worth it. You can leave now."

Luka speaks up, "We want to make up for it now. Please let us get you out of here. You don't have to have anything to do with us after that."

I shake my head, lying back down on the come-covered sheets. "I'm not worth saving, remember? I'm just a common street whore. It doesn't even matter anyway, I'm done."

Silas's brows knit together as he asks, "What the fuck is that supposed to mean?"

"I'm done trusting people. I'm done in general." I'm ripped from the bed suddenly and thrown over someone's shoulder. "Put me down!" I scream.

Jax growls out, "No."

"No? No?" I scream, sounding slightly hysterical now. "You didn't want me anymore. You treated me as if I was disposable. No, I guess I *was* disposable. For fucking information!" I pound his back with my fists, bouncing on his shoulder with each step he takes down the stairs.

We exit the house, and my feet hit the ground. I glare at the guys all around me as I demand, "What the fuck is wrong with you!?"

Jax shrugs as he responds in a nonchalant tone, "Now, you're free."

"Free?" I screech. "I have nowhere to go, and no one I can trust. What the fuck do you mean by free?" I can feel tears stinging my eyes, and I'm angry when they start streaming down my face.

"Then come home with us," Luka whispers.

I growl out each word as I say, "I. DON'T. TRUST. YOU." A clap of thunder roars after my words, really hammering home my point. I have to admit the weather is mirroring my mood perfectly right now. I turn to go back inside, but Jax blocks my path. "Move!"

Jax shakes his head. "You don't have to trust us, but we want you safe and away from Marvin. Come home."

All of my anger and fire disappears just as quickly as it appeared, and the bone-deep exhaustion I've felt the last few weeks returns. I look up at him as tears continue to stream down my face. "I'm so tired, Jax."

His brows knit together as he says, "Let's go home then, Mace."

He doesn't understand. I shake my head as I try to explain, "I'm tired of trusting. I'm tired of being betrayed. I'm tired of living." I begin to sob. Every feeling and emotion I have held back for the last fifteen-odd years collides inside of me. I wipe at my face as I whisper, "I can't do this anymore, Jax."

Jax steps forward, frowning. "Come on, little wolf cub. Wolves don't give up. We keep fighting."

"I don't want to fight anymore," I hiccup out.

Luka steps up beside me, and I take a step back. I see that he's holding my macaroni Squishmallow. He holds it out to me as he says, "You can't stop fighting now, Mac."

I grab it and shove my face into it. It smells like him, and I fall to my knees. Another loud boom of thunder sounds as my knees hit the ground. Rain starts to pour as I sob into the stuffy. I want to trust them so badly. I want to belong somewhere. I want to... to be loved. There's a squelch beside me as Luka kneels in the mud next to me. He pulls me into his lap, and I let him. I don't have the energy to fight anymore. He rocks me as I hear the others surround us. I look up and find Jax and Silas are now on the ground with us.

Strands of his long blond hair stick to Jax's face as he gives me a sad smile and says, "Don't give up, Mace."

I look at Silas, noticing his hair is a complete mess. He bites his lip and says, "It's okay if you don't trust us. But please, come home."

Lightning flashes across the sky as Luka holds me tighter. "Let us earn your trust back. Come home."

Home. That's all I've ever wanted. Somewhere I can be myself. Somewhere safe.

I must have cried myself to sleep because when I wake up, I'm in a familiar bedroom. I shift, wiping at my crusty eyes. When they are less blurry, I look around and find that they had tucked me in tightly with my macaroni Squishmallow. I smile down at the stuffy; it's my favorite gift that I have ever received.

Looking down at myself, I notice I'm still in my clothes from Marvin's house. Well, what's left of them. I wince when I notice how horrible I smell. How did the guys not cringe away from that stench? Grunting, I push myself out of bed and strip as I make my way to the attached bathroom. I twist the shower knobs to make the water as hot as I can stand and look around as the water heats up. I notice that the bathroom still looks the same as when I left.

My towel is still hanging on the same hook, and the shampoo and conditioner bottles are in the same spot. Shaking my head at the random thoughts running through my mind, I jump under the spray.

The moment the water hits me, I moan. This feels fucking amazing. I wash my hair twice to make sure I get the stench of Marvin out, reveling in the feel of how soft my hair is after I condition it. I soap up my loofa and scrub. I scrub until my skin is red. I try to scrub away Marvin's phantom fingers as he ran them over my skin. Fuck! Why the hell did I let that fucker touch and fuck me?

I shudder at the memories and shrink down in the corner of the shower, my eyes stinging with tears. Why did I give up? Why did I forget to fight? I jump when I hear a knock on the bathroom door. Looking up, I see a figure standing in the doorway. He's fuzzy due to the frosted shower glass and the steam creating fog in the room. I'm not sure who it is, so I wait.

A throat clears, and I hear, "I wanted to check on you. The shower has been running for a while."

I smile at Luka's hesitant voice. Always so sweet and considerate. I clear my throat and reply, "I'm fine."

I see his figure bob. "Right. Um... I wanted to let you know breakfast is ready. You've gotten smaller since we last... since we last saw you," his voice breaks on the last part.

"Did you know he was going to trade me for information?"

He sighs and says, "We knew he was planning on it. We argued about it the night before we went to that meeting. Jax and I didn't agree with the plan, but..." I watch through the frosted glass as he leans up against the wall beside the door. "But... but we didn't stop him. And that's on us."

They should have, but I made my point earlier. "What was the information?"

I watch as he slides down the wall. "The location of a man we've been looking for for years."

"And who is this man?"

"He was... he was the man who killed our oldest brother, Grayson. We haven't been able to find him. No matter how much we were willing to pay for intel, no one had anything. Marvin said he knew where the guy was located, but he would only give it to us if we handed you over."

So I was traded for information on the man who killed their brother? Well, that cools most of my anger about the situation. What would I do if it was my dad? What would I be willing to give? I sigh and ask, "So did you find him?"

He grunts. "We went directly to his house. Jax kicked down the door. The man was sitting in his living room lounging while a woman sucked him off. The man who murdered our brother was living it up and enjoying himself. I've never seen Silas so angry."

Well, now I'm invested. Standing up under the spray, I ask, "What do you mean?"

He sighs. "Silas likes clean kills. One shot to the head. But with him… he made that man suffer."

I touch a finger to the glass, drawing swirls in the fog from the steam. "That's understandable. The man killed your brother."

I watch Luka's figure shake as his voice grows hushed. "You don't understand. Silas used a knife and sliced the man over and over again. We had to pull him off. I don't even think he realizes it, but he was screaming and crying the whole time. He was still slicing up the guy even after he was dead. Silas was covered in blood."

I shut off the water and reach out to grab my towel. Wrapping it around myself, I open the door to look down at Luka on the ground. He looks up at me as I shrug, "Like I said, the man killed your brother."

Luka shakes his head again and slides himself up the wall until he's standing. "We've killed people before, Mac. We killed the man responsible for our father's death, and Silas didn't even bat an eye." Luka points to the center of his forehead and says, "One shot."

"Okay, so what made this different?"

He points at me. "You."

My brows knit together in confusion. "Me?"

"My brother doesn't show he cares well. He doesn't show emotion well, either. He has convinced himself that caring for anyone will only give our enemies ammo."

"He cares about you and Jax."

He shrugs. "Behind closed doors? Yes. In front of the public? The public knows we are brothers, and of course, that we care about each other. But we never let them see a chink in our armor. We are strong together and apart. But you? You were becoming his chink."

I shake my head. "He doesn't care for me in that way. He's never shown any interest in me like that. You and Jax are the only ones."

Luka smirks. "Are you sure about that?"

I'm about to argue. Yes, I'm sure, but I stop when memories of our time together surface. Silas was the one who let me use this bedroom, a bedroom away from the guys so I had a floor all to myself. He was the first one to have clothes delivered for me. He helped me pick out my dress the first time we went out. He's the one who made sure there was food for my breakfast, lunch, and dinner. And when I mentioned a favorite snack or drink, it would always be there for me the next day. I look back up to Luka wide-eyed.

He smiles knowingly, "Like I said, he doesn't show he cares well. He doesn't show he cares in physical touch or by passing words. He does manage to show it by making sure you're taken care of."

"What does that have to do with the death?" I whisper.

"The moment he handed you over, he regretted it. The only way he could get his feelings out was to take them out on the guy who killed our brother. He cares. Maybe more than Jax and I combined. He hides behind a mask of strength and indifference, and the only one to ever break it was you. You are the chink in his armor."

With that, he slips out of the bathroom, leaving me staring after him wide-eyed and mouth agape.

CHAPTER TWENTY-FIVE
MACY

After getting dressed, I slip quietly downstairs. I suddenly hear shouting and run toward the sound. When I reach the kitchen, I'm greeted by all three guys standing around the island. Silas is holding a phone up between them. He rolls his eyes before looking back down at the phone. "I don't understand the issue, Marvin."

"You stole my fucking whore!" Marvin screams from the other end of the line.

"I don't remember stealing anything. It's not my problem if your so-called whore left you," Silas sneers at the phone. I'm about to say something, but Jax holds up a hand to silence me. I frown at him, and he holds a finger to his lips with a smirk.

I turn my gaze to Luka. He smiles softly, mouthing, "Trust us."

I huff out a sigh but decide to play along as I make my way to the island and take a seat on one of the high-top stools. Silas turns away and grabs something from behind him. Turning back to me, he slides me a plate, surprising me.

He taps beside the plate and mouths, "Eat it all."

I roll my eyes, but I can't stop the smile that crosses my lips as I look down at the french toast. I love his french toast. He's come leaps and bounds from only being able to cook eggs and bacon. He even learned to make the bread himself. There's a pang in my chest when I realize that he learned to cook after noticing how I only snacked when food was placed in front of me.

Next to the french toast, there's bacon along with some strawberries and cream. I take a bite and have to bite my lip to fight back a moan. I don't want to ruin whatever this conversation is about, but fuck this food is amazing. My eyes meet Silas's, and he's smirking. I have a feeling this is his peace offering. Not wanting to give him the satisfaction, I open my mouth to show him all my chewed up food. He snorts out a laugh.

"What the fuck is going on?" Marvin yells from the other side of the phone.

Silas's eyes harden again as he snaps, "None of your fucking business. As I was saying, we don't have your fucking whore."

I raise a brow in question, but Silas ignores me. My eyes shift from his when a large cup of coffee is placed beside my plate. I look up to find Jax mouthing, "Your favorite."

I take the cup and inhale. Fuck, I love coffee. I've missed it. I take a sip and look back at Jax to find him smacking a box of smokes on the counter. I thought he quit smoking. I put the cup down and cover his hand with mine. His eyes widen as they meet mine. I look back down at the box and then back up at him in question. He sighs, whispering, "You were gone." My eyes widen at his admission. I look back over to Luka and remember our conversation while I was in the shower. It seems my absence affected them more than I thought.

I squeeze Jax's hand before letting go. "I'm here now," I whisper back.

He looks at me for a moment before nodding. He continues to smack the counter with the box but doesn't take a cigarette out. I focus back on my food and Silas's conversation.

"I know you took her. You are the only people who could have walked into my house without my people alerting me."

"We took Macy, not your whore."

"It's the same fucking thing!" Marvin screams.

Jax growls. "No, it's not!"

"She belongs to me while her father owes me money."

Silas grins in triumph as he replies, "Funny, you should mention that. We looked into the father. Seems her father cleaned up and hasn't bought from you in three years. You told her father that you released Macy, and she ran off to another state to start a new life."

I choke on my food, and Luka has to smack me on the back to dislodge it. I look up at Silas wide-eyed, and I can see the apology in his eyes as he continues talking, "Seems you've been keeping her as an escort for no reason."

Marvin growls on the other end, "I needed to make my money back somehow. Her useless father thought it was honorable to stop gambling money he didn't have. Thought his daughter was more important."

"So you admit that you kept Macy only to make money?" Jax questions.

"Why the fuck wouldn't I? She's my highest-paid escort. I'm making more money off of her than I do any of my other girls."

Silas continues talking as if Marvin hadn't spoken, "We also looked into finding her father. How did you make him disappear?"

"I killed him a year ago when I caught him snooping around. He didn't believe me when I said she went off to college in another state."

I cover my mouth to dampen my scream. He killed my dad? My dad is dead? He's... dead. I look into Silas's eyes. He mouths, "I'm sorry."

I shake my head as my vision becomes blurry. It's not his fault. It's Marvin's. Jax and Luka come up beside me and wrap their arms around me.

Silas grunts. "I don't think you realize what you've done."

"What the fuck is that little whore going to do? I'm not afraid of her."

Silas's eyes meet mine as he says, "You forget that she's one of us now."

"Oh, is she spreading her legs for you now? She's such a fucking whore. Do you enjoy the way her cunt clamps down—"

"Enough," Silas yells as he slams a hand on the counter. I can't do anything but stare at him, eyes wide. His eyes darken so much that they are almost black, and he's breathing heavily as he lowers his voice. His tone is deadly as he says, "She commands wolves now, I would watch your back."

"The fuck is that supposed to mean?"

Silas's smile is that of a wolf's as he sneers and warns, "Beware the hunt." Then he ends the call before Marvin can say anything else.

Silas

My phone starts ringing, and I growl as I look down to see who it is. It better not be that fucker again. I freeze when I see Jane's name. Why would she be calling? She hardly ever calls. Sliding my thumb across the screen, I answer, "Jane?"

"What the fuck did you do?" she screeches through the phone.

I press the speakerphone button so my brothers can hear what's going on. "What do you mean?"

"What did you do to my friend?"

My eyes look up to find Macy bringing a cup of coffee to her lips. I can see the tilt of a smirk as she stares back at me unblinkingly. I sigh, running a hand through my hair. Checkmate. I see what you did there. I can't even be mad at her, either. "She's sitting right here in front of me. I have you on speaker if you want to talk to her."

"You damn well know it's not her I want to talk to. I've already spoken to her which is why I'm calling you! Must I repeat myself before you answer the question?" she yells down the line.

I grind my teeth and ask, "If you already know what happened, then why are you asking?"

"I want to know what was running through your head when you decided to betray her. I want to know what that betrayal was worth to you."

I look up to find Macy watching me. Her eyes are guarded as if she's afraid of my answer. I huff out a sigh and say, "I just wanted vengeance for my brother."

I hear Jane sigh on the other end. "Did you get it?"

"Yes," I whisper. I know what her next question will be, and the answer scares me to be honest.

"Was it worth it?"

I shift my eyes down to the phone because I can't look Macy in the eyes as I answer. "No." It wasn't. I gained nothing by killing that man. It didn't bring back my brother, and it didn't give me the satisfaction I was looking for. What it brought me was a gut full of regret because I betrayed the only woman to ever look at my brother's and I as men. We weren't prizes or beasts to her. Just men. That's all.

Jane sighs and says, "You three are lucky you're family."

"I know," I grit out, still refusing to look at Macy.

Jane hums. "Jace talked me out of shoving a rod up your dick hole and cutting off your balls."

My hand automatically shifts to my dick to protect it. I hear a choking sound and looking up, I find Luka patting Macy on the back. Her eyes are wide as saucers as she looks at me. I can't stop the tilt to my lips as I shrug. This is mild torture for Jane. "I'll make sure to thank Jace the next time I see him."

She hums again. "You do that. Now, I expect you to treat that woman like a queen from now on. If I hear you have betrayed her again, I will follow through on my threat. Jace won't be able to stop me next time."

"Understood."

Jane groans as she says, "I have to go. The baby doesn't like all the stress you've caused me."

Jax speaks up for the first time. "Make sure you rest."

"Yeah, yeah. Bye." The line suddenly goes dead as we all look at the phone.

It's quiet for a moment before Macy speaks up, "So am I in trouble for using my badass bestie against you guys?"

"No, it was well deserved," Luka says from beside her.

Guess now is as good a time as any. I turn from the island and open a drawer. I pull out a set of keys before turning back around. I had these made awhile back, but I wasn't sure if I wanted to give them to her or not. I think it's time. I hold them out to her. "These are for you."

She looks at them before looking back up at me. "What are those?"

I jingle them before saying, "They are keys to this building. You now have a key for the downstairs door as well as a key to access each level of the building in case of a lockdown. There is also a key to one of the cars downstairs for you to use, if you would like."

Her eyes widen for a moment before narrowing. "Is this your way of buying my time again so this stays transactional?"

I flinch at her words, even though they're justified. "No. This is my way of showing you that you are welcome to come and go as you please. This is now your home as much as it is ours."

Her eyes are still narrowed and full of suspicion as she says, "I'm not sure if I should believe you or not."

I nod in understanding and come around the island as I say, "I have something to show you." My brothers stand to follow me. She looks between us warily before doing the same. We make our way to the elevator, and I press the level for her floor once everyone is inside.

Once the doors open, I lead the way down the hall. I look over my shoulder to watch Macy's face as we pass the room she has been staying in. Her brows furrow in confusion as she follows. "Where are we going?"

I wait until we reach a closed door before turning to face her. With my hand on the handle I answer, "Your new bedroom." I twist the knob, letting the door swing open.

She arches a brow at me before entering the room. I know she's surprised by the gasp she lets out as she takes in the space. I thought she would have noticed that all of her things were gone from her bedroom last night, but she didn't. My brothers had snuck into her room and brought everything in here.

This is the room I had been renovating for her before I agreed to hand her back to Marvin. The bathroom is completely new, and I knocked out a wall in the adjoining room to make a large walk-in closet. The back wall is all bookshelves, and Jax had gone snooping through her e-reader to find the books she liked.

When she was back with Marvin, he had gone out and bought every book from her e-reader. Including all of the special editions. Luka had bought large Squishmallows to lay in the corner where she could read. He also bought a few fluffy rugs and blankets for the reading nook.

"What is all of this?" she whispers.

Jax comes up beside her, slipping his fingers though hers as he says, "We wanted you to have your own room. A place to call your own."

"I find it hard to believe you did all of this overnight."

Luka steps up to her other side, also slipping his hand into hers. "We've actually been working on this room for a while."

She looks over her shoulder to find me. Biting her lip, she asks, "Then why did you send me back?"

Sighing, I walk up to her, pressing a kiss to her forehead before backing away. "Because... I'm afraid. And fear makes people do stupid things." I turn, walking out the door. I need to leave. If I stay any longer I will say something I don't deserve to.

Once in the elevator, I press the level for the gym. Maybe if I release some of this tension inside, it will lessen the ache in my chest.

CHAPTER TWENTY-SIX
MACY

"Where is he going?" I ask, confused at why he walked away.

Luka sighs and replies, "To the gym."

I look between Luka and Jax, wondering why they both have the same sad look on their faces. "What's with the faces? What am I missing?"

Jax sighs before saying, "He's building up his walls again. "

I arch a brow in question. This time Luka speaks up. "The only person he has ever allowed to see him... the real him, since our brother died, is Jane."

Now that I think about it, I realize he's only ever smiled when he was around her or talking to her. Not the fake smiles he gives everyone else but a real smile. Luka continues, "But you... you are shattering those walls, Mac. He was just a ghost with a beating heart... until you. He's trying to take a step back so he can rebuild them."

"Why is he trying to build them back?"

Luka sends me a wistful smile as he says, "You are his chink."

My eyes widen with realization before I'm squeezing out from between them. I run toward the stairs, skipping a few steps as I make my way to the gym. I'm out of breath by the time I bust through the door of the home gym, and I take a second to catch my breath. Silas doesn't even notice me as he punches the bag in the center of the room with his headphones on. As I walk closer, I notice he didn't tape his knuckles. Blood is dripping on the floor as he continues to punch the bag.

I walk around so I can see his face. He still doesn't notice me, his focus completely on the bag in front of him. I'm still a little out of breath when I look into his dark hazel eyes. They are filled with so much pain and self-loathing. I move a little closer, and the movement startles him out of his thoughts. He grabs the bag, stopping its motion before ripping off his headphones. "What the fuck are you doing down here?"

His words, though biting, aren't filled with the normal anger and iciness I've come to expect from him. I realize now that that was a front to push me away, but why?

"I came to check on you." I point down to his hands. "You're bleeding. You should have worn wraps."

He glances down at his hands before looking back up at me with a shrug. "I'm fine. You can go back to the others."

I go to reach for him, but he backs away, shaking his head. "Don't touch me."

I don't reach out again, but I do step closer. "Let me help with your hands, Silas."

He shakes his head again, looking at the ground. "I'll be fine. Just go." I know he meant for his words to come out cold, to further push me away, but I can hear the desperation in them. Blood continues to drip from his fingers before he curls them into fists. His body shakes as he continues to pant, looking down at the ground.

"Silas," I whisper. "What's wrong?"

When he looks up at me, I let out a gasp. His eyes are filled with so much fear and desperation. "You... you make me feel, Macy. You make me feel too much."

I open my mouth to say something... anything, but he shakes his head and says, "I don't like it... I need it to stop. Now... I need it to stop."

His body shakes harder as he looks back to the floor. I look at him. Really look at him. I see it now. He's shattering. He's built his walls so thick around him so that no one could hurt him again. He loved his brother fiercely and lost him. I think of my father, and tears sting my eyes. Silas's brother was murdered years ago, and he's carried that pain... that grief for years. He wasn't satisfied with killing the man who murdered his brother because it didn't bring him back.

I reach for him but freeze because what can I say? Biting my lip, I force out the words, "It's okay to care about someone."

He shakes his head. "I can't. I'll fail in some way. I won't be able to protect you. I've already failed you once; who's to say I won't do it again. I will do it again."

"Who says I need protecting?"

He looks up at me, his tormented eyes meeting mine. "They will use you like they used Jane. I can't do it, Macy. I almost lost her." His voice cracks and then shakes as he says, "I had to watch as she almost bled to death because I failed to protect her. I was the one who rescued her when she was kidnapped. I saw her broken and bruised body. I watched as she broke. I held her in my arms as she sobbed."

He reaches up to cup both sides of my face. "I can't do it, Macy." I watch as this man... the strongest and fiercest man I know, fractures into thousands of pieces right in front of me. "I'm not... I'm not strong enough."

I see the years of responsibility weighing down his shoulders. Of making sure his family stayed safe while holding everyone at a distance.

I reach up slowly, as if he were a wild animal. As if any sudden movement would scare him away. I cup the side of his sweaty cheek and watch as his eyes flutter closed. I caress his cheek, noticing now the dark circles under his eyes. The slight bruising to his jaw and the cut on his lip. This man, who tries to make it appear as if he cares about nothing and no one, in reality cares so deeply for those he deems worthy. He protects and loves so fiercely.

His eyes squeeze together as he takes a shuddering breath. His voice is only a whisper as he says, "I could lose everything. My money, my cars, even my empire. But you?" His eyes flutter open and spear me with their intensity. I watch his dark thoughts swirl behind his hazel eyes as they dim.

With his next words, his eyes fill with unshed tears. "I couldn't lose you." He presses his forehead to mine as he whispers, "Fucking hell... not you." Squeezing his eyes shut, he pulls away. My own eyes widen as I see tears slide down his face, and he turns away. "I tried so hard. So fucking hard not to care. To push you away with every harsh word I possessed." He lets out a bitter wet laugh. "But no matter what I did, you still broke down those carefully constructed walls."

I don't think; I just grab him, turning him towards me. I slam my lips to his, tasting the saltiness of his tears as we kiss. It takes a moment before his lips move against mine, but then he's kissing me like a starving man.

He pulls away suddenly, and I look up at him with an arched brow. "What's wrong?"

His eyes are no longer sad but filled with need and want. "What's wrong?" He's panting as his forehead presses against mine. "If I didn't pull away... I wouldn't have been able to stop kissing you."

I smile as I softly brush my lips against his again. He groans and I say, "Who says I want you to stop?"

CHAPTER TWENTY-SEVEN
MACY

Silas' lips brush against mine as he says, "I don't deserve your kisses."

He's right. He doesn't deserve my kisses, but fuck if I am going to walk away without kissing him. Without tasting the need and want on his lips. Luka was right; he does want me. Though from what he shared with me, it's more than want. He needs me. Maybe as much as I need him.

His thumb continues to caress my cheek as my fingers slide into his hair. Our foreheads still touch as we breathe each other in. I don't want this moment to end. I don't want it to shatter into a million pieces because I feel like this version of Silas will disappear when it does. This moment is important.

My voice is soft as I say, "Tell me you're sorry."

The hand he has on my back curls into a fist as his breath catches. He begins to pull away, but my hand tightens in his hair as I say again, "Tell me you're sorry."

His eyes meet mine briefly before they close tight, his face wet with sweat and tears. His forehead bumps mine softly as he lets out a shuddering breath. "I can never express how sorry I am."

He pulls away as he opens his hazel eyes, wet with sorrow. They meet mine as he cups my face and says, "Words cannot convey how much I regret my actions. I will spend eternity showing you just how sorry I am."

His eyes stay on mine as he rests his forehead on mine once more. "But I will say it again and again and again. I'm sorry." His voice cracks.

My fingers tighten in his hair as I say, "The three of you made me care." I swallow the lump in my throat as I try to keep my emotions from spilling out. "You made me care," I whisper and release my hold on his hair as I lower my arms to wrap around his abdomen.

He lowers his hands from my face to wrap around my shoulders, pulling me close. I feel his chest rumble and he rasps, "I'm sorry."

My eyes burn as I wrap my arms tighter around him. I should feel grossed out by the fact that my face is in his sweaty tank, but everything is forgotten at this moment. My voice wavers as I say, "I knew the day would come when I would have to go back. But I didn't want it to. Least of all like that."

His fingers slip through my hair, holding my head closer to him as his lips brush the top of my head. "I'm sorry."

I thought I had cried the last of my tears last night, but I guess not. I squeeze my eyes shut as they slip through. "I wanted to stay here forever," I say brokenly.

His body begins to shake as his lips brush against the top of my head. "I'm sorry," he whispers again.

I hiccup as a sob breaks through. "This was home," I say through my tears.

His breathing turns ragged as he holds me tight. His voice is deep and brittle as he says, "I'm... sorry..."

My fingers dig into his shirt. "Don't throw me away again. Please," I whimper.

He grunts as he says, "Never again."

I tighten my hold on him as I plead, "Promise?"

I feel his body shudder as he takes a deep breath. "Promise, little wolf."

My words are muffled as I whisper, "I forgive you."

His body stiffens, and I feel him shake his head. "I don't deserve that, little wolf."

"Don't break your promise, and all is forgiven."

He lets out a choked sound as his body continues to shake. "Don't forgive me yet."

"You have it as long as you don't break your promise."

He pulls away. "Look at me." Pulling my face away from his chest, I look up. His cheeks are tear stained, and his eyes are red rimmed. They rove over my face before meeting my gaze. His eyes are unwaveringly serious as he vows, "I will never break that promise."

Uncoiling my arms from around him, I cup his cheeks. His eyes flutter shut for a moment before opening again. His gaze never wavers from mine as I say, "I forgive you."

His face contorts, as if tortured by my words. "I don't deserve your forgiveness."

"It's my trust you need to earn more than my forgiveness."

The tip of his tongue darts out, wetting his lips. "How?" he asks almost desperately.

I'm not sure how to answer him. No one has ever wanted to earn my trust, let alone earn it back once lost. To be honest, I know the others want me here. It's always been Silas that I've questioned. "Tell me you want me to stay. Show me you want me here. I don't want to be tossed aside again."

He nods. "I can do that."

"You sure?" I whisper.

Pressing a kiss to my forehead, he whispers back, "I want you to stay. Stay here with us. Please. With... me. Let us show you what it means to be a family."

My chest warms at his words. Family? It's been a long time since I've had a family. The only family I ever had was my dad. Suddenly, it's like a bucket of cold water is thrown over that warm feeling. My dad. He's dead.

He must see the tears welling in my eyes. "Macy?"

A sob clogs my throat as I choke out, "Dad."

His eyes widen in realization. He pulls me to his chest, holding me close. "I'm sorry. I'm so sorry, Macy. I didn't want you to find out that way."

I shake my head as I continue to cry. "I... needed... to know."

He continues to hold me close as he tries to soothe me. I hear his whispered words that I'm sure I'm not supposed to hear. "Fuck. Your tears make me want to rip that man apart."

My watery chuckle sounds distorted as I say, "As long as I can help."

He grunts. "Of course."

"He doesn't even have a grave for me to visit," I say mournfully.

"We'll make him one."

I sigh. "You don't—"

He interrupts, "His soul deserves a place to rest even if there isn't a body."

Holding him tightly, I say softly, "Thank you."

"No thanks needed, little wolf."

I snort out a laugh. "Little wolf? Shouldn't I be the moon or something considering I'm Selene, right?"

He's silent for a moment, and I'm a bit worried that I've said something wrong. I'm about to say *I was joking* when he finally speaks. His voice is rough as he says, "I will call you my moon when I have earned your trust."

I hum thoughtfully at his words. I'll look forward to the day then.

CHAPTER TWENTY-EIGHT
MACY

It feels like we've been holding each other in the silence of the gym for hours. Then I remember his bruised and bloody knuckles. Pulling away, I immediately grab his hands, my eyes wide as I take in the damage.

I look up to meet his eyes as I say, "We should probably get your hands fixed up."

He shrugs as he tries to pull his hand from mine. "I've had worse."

Shaking my head, I turn to head toward the elevator, keeping his hand in mine. I pull him with me as I say, "We still need to fix them up. I should have a first aid kit in my bathroom."

"You really don't have to do this," he argues.

I look over my shoulder with a soft smile. "I know. But I want to."

His eyes widen for a moment before they soften. He nods and follows me into the elevator. It's quiet as we make our way up to my level. Quiet but not an uncomfortable silence. He breaks the silence as the elevator door opens. "There's a kit in your new bathroom. I'm sure they guys moved all your stuff over while you were dealing with me."

I snort out a laugh. "Dealing with you?"

He shrugs. "I know, I'm difficult."

I hum as I drag him along. "I would say stubborn, not difficult. You're also extremely misunderstood."

He huffs out a laugh. "Misunderstood?"

I snicker. "Yes, misunderstood." With a smile, I walk through the doorway of my new bedroom to find Jax and Luka have already made themselves comfortable on my new bed. My heart warms as I take a good look around, noticing that there is a sapphire blue accent wall. The rest of the room is painted a soft cream with matching blue accessories.

The guys look up from their spots on the bed. Jax is lying on his stomach as he reads a book, and Luka is lying against the headboard, snuggling several Squishmallows.

Jax's eyes flick between Silas and me before he asks, "Good talk?"

I laugh as I move to the bathroom. "The talk went fine. Seems your brother forgot to put wraps on and messed up his knuckles, though."

Jax hums from his position on the bed. "Doesn't seem like a Silas thing to do."

Silas grunts as he follows. "I was... distracted."

Luka snorts. "Yeah, I'm sure you were distracted."

I feel Silas stiffen, so I stop whatever is about to happen before it can start. "Boys, enough. I'm going to nurse him back to health. Continue making yourself at home in my room."

"Will do," Luka says as he snuggles back down.

"Nurse him real good, Sweets," Jax says with a laugh as I roll my eyes, shutting the door behind me.

Shaking my head, I look for the first aid kit. I search the same spot where it was in the other bathroom and grin when I find it. Setting it on the counter, I hop up to sit next to it. Silas is still standing next to the shut door.

Smirking, I crook my finger at him, beckoning him over. "Come on, Si. I promise I won't bite."

Seeing the tilt to his lips as he makes his way over warms my heart. It's a real smile. I feel my cheeks heat as he offers me his hand. Pulling out the gauze, I wet it with some iodine. I wince as I clean the raw areas on the knuckles. "Sorry," I whisper.

"I've had worse, dear."

I try to be gentle as I continue to clean his cuts. "I'm sure, but I bet it still stings."

He hums. "It does, but it's not the worst pain I've had."

Unsure what to say in response, I make sure I've thoroughly cleaned each knuckle before applying some cream on the raw spots. Placing the now clean and nursed hand on my thigh, I reach for the other one.

"What did you mean by misunderstood?" Silas asks in a soft voice.

Concentrating on his knuckles and hand, I say, "I feel like people see the persona you display, and they don't often stick around long enough to notice it's a mask."

The hand on my thigh lowers to the edge of my knee as his thumb begins caressing my leg. "A mask?"

I nod as I say, "Yeah. You display an emotionless mask of distance and indifference. You let people believe that you don't feel."

I bite my lip, as I try to not hurt his knuckles. It's hard considering I'm trying to get a stubborn bit of dirt out of the raw gashes. I can feel his eyes boring into me, so I look up to meet his soft gaze. "What?"

He smiles as he says, "You sound like her."

Brows bunching in confusion, I ask, "Her?"

"You sound like Jane."

I snort out a laugh as my focus shifts back to his hand. "She's way cooler than I am. Don't think I could ever sound like her. She also has that aura of silent danger about her. I would probably piss myself if I were stuck in a room with her not knowing who she was."

His laugh is booming as he says, "She does have that look of complete innocence, then kills you before you realize she's dangerous."

"Right? She scared the hell out of me when I first met her. I thought she was going to kill me in her basement."

He continues to laugh. "I wouldn't have let her kill you."

I arch a disbelieving brow. "I doubt that. You disliked me at the time. I'm sure you would have helped her hide the body."

He shakes his head with a smile. "I might have acted like I disliked you, but in all reality, I liked you more than I wanted to admit."

Humming, I apply the cream to his knuckles. "If you say so."

His grip on my thigh tightens for a moment before he continues caressing my leg. "I do."

I smile as I hold up his hand, twisting it from side to side. "I think your hands will be good as new in a few days."

He leans forward, brushing a kiss on my forehead. "Thank you, dear."

Wrapping my legs around him, I pull him closer to wrap my arms around his abdomen. My head rests under his chin as I hug him. "You're welcome."

After a moment of hesitation, he wraps his arms around me, holding me back. "I'm not much of a hugger or cuddler."

Humming against his chest, I smile. "I think you're doing just fine. Does this bother you?"

"No," he whispers.

His arms tighten around me as he rests his head on top of mine. He lets out a sigh and I ask, "Touch starved?"

"Maybe."

"You can have a hug whenever you want."

His voice is muffled as he says, "I'm out of practice. I don't want to ask for something you wouldn't want to give."

I smile as I cuddle closer. "I'm willing to give hugs whenever you want or need them. You don't have to ask."

"Can we stay like this for a few moments longer?" he whispers.

"Of course." I had a feeling that he wouldn't be the one to initiate physical touch. He doesn't feel comfortable enough with our dynamic to do that. I will have to be the one to initiate physical touch for a while. He's also the one I feel needs physical touch the most.

There's a soft knock on the bathroom door, and Silas stiffens. I rub his back as I say quietly, "It's okay." Then I yell, "Yes?"

Luka answers, "I wanted to check-in. You've been in there for a bit."

I hear Jax yell, "I told him that you were *nursing* Silas back to health." He put heavy emphasis on nursing.

I snort out a laugh and yell back, "He's good to go. We are just talking. Do you need me?"

"I wanted to check-in. No hurry."

Silas groans into my hair. "I should probably let you spend some time with them." He pulls away, looking down at me with a sad smile. "You were closer to them than me. I'm sure they are worried. I shouldn't take up all your time."

I tug on the neck of his shirt before he can get too far. Pressing my lips lightly against his, I pull away. "No more purposefully staying away, okay?"

He huffs out a sigh. "Right. I'll try."

I can tell he's emotionally exhausted. But I don't want him rebuilding the walls I've managed to break down. "Don't hide away from me again. Please."

His gaze softens as he leans in to press a kiss to my forehead. "I'm heading up to my office to get some work done. I'm not hiding. If you want to come up, you're more than welcome."

I smile as I say, "I may take you up on that. I can come up anytime?"

He caresses my cheek before pulling away. Heading toward the closed door he looks over his shoulder. "Anytime, dear."

My smile is wide as he opens the door and walks out. Standing on the other side is Luka. He looks between the two of us before his gaze settles back on me. "Why are you smiling so much, Mac?"

I hop off the counter, taking his hand in mine as we head over to my bed. "He trusts me."

Jax arches a brow as he asks, "What do you mean?"

Hopping onto the bed, I settle between the two of them. "He said I could come up to the office whenever I want."

Luka hums as I lean my head on his shoulder. "I think he's always trusted you, Mac. He didn't want you involved in what we have to deal with, though."

Jax flips onto his other side to begin massaging one of my feet. I hum as I close my eyes. "He doesn't mind me getting involved now?"

Jax gives my foot a squeeze before saying, "He sees you as a member of the pack now. No reason to hide anything if it could cost you your life."

I groan when Jax hits a sore spot. I snuggle into Luka as I relax between them. Yawning, I say, "That makes sense."

"Sleepy, Mace?"

"It's too early to take a nap," I mumble.

"Never too early for a nap," Luka says as he places my macaroni squish in my lap.

I hum as I snuggle with my noodle and Luka. I try to fight the yawn, but it's too powerful. "Will you guys be here when I wake up?"

I feel the bed dip as Jax flips around so he's now leaning against the headboard on my other side. I feel his heat seep into me as his hand rests against my thigh. Caressing in small circles, he asks, "Do you want us to be here?"

I can feel myself falling into the depths of sleep as I mumble, "Yes."

Luka rests a hand on my other thigh as he says, "Then we will be."

Darkness quickly takes over as exhaustion consumes me. I can't stop the feeling of contentment and safety I feel as their warmth surrounds me. I may not have said it, but I forgave them too.

CHAPTER TWENTY-NINE
MACY

"I love you!"

I stand, mouth agape, as I stare at Luka. He's holding out a new Squishmallow, but it's his wide eyes that have me trying to find my bearings. Did... did he just say he loved me?

I watch as his panic sets in. "Shit! Um... fuck, I didn't mean for that to slip out."

It's been a week since my return to their house, and my relationship with Jax and Luka has slowly started to recover. They haven't pushed for anything and gladly savor my attention when I give it. We also haven't had sex since I've been back. Not that they've pushed for it, but I also don't exactly know how to get that intimacy back.

It takes me a moment before I slowly reach out for the Squishmallow. "You... You love me?"

He runs his fingers through his short hair, gripping it with frustration as he looks anywhere but at me. "I'm sorry! I don't know why that slipped out. I mean, I've been thinking about it, but I didn't want to overwhelm you. I've been in love with you for a while now. Since before... before the incident. Though, I'm sure that seems unbelievable considering what we did..."

I interrupt his rambling by placing a finger over his lips. His wide, panicked eyes meet mine as I smile. "You love me?"

His eyes flick between mine before he gives me a nod. "Yes."

My eyes begin to burn as my smile widens. Is this... is this what love feels like? My chest feels heavy but not in a bad way. It feels like it's full.

His thumb brushes across my cheek as his eyes shift from panic to worry. "Mac? Mac, please, don't cry."

A sob slips through as I quietly say, "No one... no one has said they loved me before."

He pulls me into his arms, holding me close. "I do," he whispers.

I want to believe him. So badly. Actions speak louder than words, they say, and I've seen his actions. He's shown how much he cares for me. But, words are important too. Words hold just as much power. "Say it again."

"I love you, Macy," he says softly, pulling away just enough to look down. The sincerity in his eyes leaves me breathless. "The sun will always chase the moon. I'll chase after you till our dying breath. Until we are nothing but dust among the stars."

He presses a soft kiss to my forehead and whispers, "And even then. Even when we are among the stars, I'll find you. I'll always find you, Mac."

I don't mean to say it, but the words slip out. "I love you, too."

His eyes widen for a moment before they soften. "You don't have to say it back. I hadn't meant to say it myself, but since I did, I wanted to explain. I want you to know that you mean more to me than a fun fling. I want to be with you."

Rising on tiptoes, I press my lips to his. It's the first kiss I've given him since the incident, and it feels fucking amazing. His hand slips up to hold my cheek as he kisses me back softly.

My hand slides between us, and I thread my fingers through his hair to pull him closer. He groans as his other hand slips into my long tresses. My eyes fly open when my other hand caresses his cheek and finds it wet.

I pull away, breathless. "Luka?"

He squeezes his eyes closed tightly as he sucks in a breath. "I fucking missed you. I fucking missed you so much, Mac."

Wet, hazel eyes flutter open to meet mine, and his voice comes out shaky as he says, "I'm so sorry. I'm sorry I didn't stop him, Mac."

"Luka," I say softly.

He pulls away, shaking his head as he angrily wipes at his face. But the tears don't stop. "I don't deserve your love! I don't deserve your kisses! I haven't earned your trust."

I reach out for him, but he backs away even further. "Luka... I've already forgiven you guys."

"Why?!" he yells, "Why? We deserve your anger, your hatred. What we did to you was betrayal. We betrayed you!"

"I understand why you did it, Luka. I can't even say I wouldn't have done the same thing if I were in your situation."

He lets out a self-deprecating laugh. "You shouldn't be so understanding. We deserve your anger, but all you've been is understanding. You have offered your affection, and we have been greedily taking it."

"It's not like you have been forcing me to give you affection, Luka. I've wanted to do everything."

"We don't deserve it!" he shouts.

I look at him. Really look at him like I did Silas. I'm realizing that these men are more alike than they want to believe. I can see it in his eyes. The desperation for my forgiveness but not feeling worthy of it. The anger at himself for not standing up against his brother. His tears aren't only out of sadness but anger at himself.

That's when it clicks. I really mean something to him. He meant every single word he said. I need to channel my inner Selene. What would she do if one of her subjects betrayed her? I look up when a figure darkens the doorframe.

Jax stands there confused. He's looking between me and Luka. He must have heard his brother's shouting and came to figure out what was going on. Luka's shadowed eyes are still on me as I look between him and Jax.

I look around my room and smirk when I find the crown from the night we went to the club. Feeling their eyes on me, I make my way over to it and place it on my head. I turn back to them as I stand taller. I'm not Macy right now; I'm Selene.

I look at both of them before commanding, "Kneel."

Jax smirks before stepping into the room. He doesn't hesitate, falling to his knees in front of me. His eyes close, and he shivers when my fingers caress his cheek. My eyes shift to Luka who's still standing. I arch a brow as I ask, "Do I need to repeat myself?"

His voice cracks as he asks, "What are you doing?"

"Doing what I must. You seem to think you need to be punished." I look down at Jax as his green-hazel eyes meet mine. "Do you need to be punished, Jax?"

His voice is hoarse as he replies, "Yes."

I was right. They need this. My eyes drift back to Luka. "Kneel."

His eyes jump to Jax, then back to me. He slowly steps in front of me, but he doesn't fall to his knees like Jax, instead he bends to one knee before lowering the other.

I rest a hand on top of each of their heads, letting my fingers twist in their hair and tighten my grip. They both let out a hiss as I say, "Good boys."

Jax's eyes glitter with need as Luka looks at me hesitantly. I allow a smirk to grace my face as I say, "Now, show your goddess how much you need her forgiveness."

"How?" Jax croaks.

My smile grows. "Beg."

Jax's eyes widen as he turns to look at Luka, but Luka's eyes stay on me. I know I will be holding them both in my arms by the end of this, but they need to feel like they have earned my forgiveness. I have to be harsh. I have to be hateful.

I let my eyes harden as I glare down at Luka. My voice is bitter as I bark, "Beg!"

He jumps as he whispers, "I'm sorry."

I tut as I say, "That doesn't sound like begging. Do you even want my forgiveness?"

"Yes," he replies. His voice is a bit stronger now.

"Do you want my love?"

His eyes widen at that. "Yes."

"Do you think you deserve either of those things?"

He begins to tremble as he replies, "No."

"Then beg for it," I growl.

"Mace," Jax says hesitatingly.

He must see something in my gaze because he flinches when my eyes meet his. "It's not yet your turn. Be a good boy and stay quiet." He nods, looking down at the ground.

With my fingers still tangled in Luka's hair, I tug. He hisses as his eyes snap up to meet mine. "I'm not hearing anything."

His voice wobbles as he says, "I'm sorry, please forgive me."

My reply comes out scathing. "Not good enough. Did you not mean it when you said you loved me?"

His eyes widen as they meet mine. "I meant every word."

"Then why don't you sound sincere when you plead for my forgiveness? Should I doubt your words of love as well?"

"I love you! I love you more than anything!" he yells.

I arch a brow. "Then make me believe it. Make me feel the truth of your words."

My grip on Jax loosens when Luka shuffles forward. His hands rest on my hips as he looks up at me pleadingly. "I'm sorry. I'm so sorry that I didn't stop him. I'm sorry I didn't come for you. I'm sorry..." his voice breaks. He takes a deep breath before continuing, "I'm sorry that he hurt you. I'm sorry I didn't kill him."

I feel myself wavering. The utter devastation in his eyes makes me want to drop to my knees and hold him here and now, but I can't yet. He needs to feel like I've truly forgiven him. I see the tears gathering in his eyes, and I almost break. I don't want to hurt him... any of them.

His grip on my hips tightens as he takes a deep breath. "I'm sorry that I love you. I'm sorry that I broke your heart. I'm sorry, my moon. My guiding light. I'm so fucking sorry!"

His forehead drops to my abdomen as he sobs. He wraps his arms around my hips, pulling me close. My fingers brush through his hair as I whisper, "I forgive you, Luka. I did a while ago. I may be your moon, but you are the sun. My sun. I love you."

His arms tighten around me, and I continue to hold him while he breaks.

CHAPTER THIRTY
MACY

After a few minutes, my eyes drift to Jax. His eyes are still on Luka, his hands clenched tightly into fists. "Jax?"

He refuses to look at me, continuing to stare at Luka, his breathing jagged.

I add a bit more authority to my voice as I command, "Jax!"

He jumps but still refuses to look at me. Huffing out a sigh, I realize that I'm going to have to force him to meet my gaze. But first, I need to make sure Luka is okay. I shift in his hold a bit to lower myself enough to whisper in his ear, "I need to help Jax now. Are you okay, babe?"

His voice is raw as he says, "To be honest, I'm not sure."

I lower myself even more as he sits back onto his heels. I'm now in his lap as he engulfs me in a hug, his face nestled in the crook of my neck. I wrap my arms around him and hold him close as he tries to get his emotions back under control.

"I love you," I whisper.

He shivers as his arms tighten around me. His voice is muffled as he says, "I love you more."

I huff out a laugh. After a few more minutes pass, I say, "I need to help Jax, now."

"I don't want to leave," he whispers.

"You don't have to. You can wait on the bed for me. We can have a cuddle session after, how does that sound?"

His arms tighten around me before loosening. He pulls away to look down at me, "I need cuddles for sure."

I press my lips to his softly before saying, "Then cuddles you will get."

His eyes shift over to Jax before he sighs. "I'll leave you to fix my brother."

I smile as I stand. "Nothing to fix. I like you both the way you are."

He snorts out a laugh. "You'd be the first."

I smack his butt as he walks toward the bed. "And I'll be the last," I sing.

He collapses on the bed. "Good."

I shift my attention to Jax. I need to do something different with him. Making my way over to him, I kneel down in front of him. Lifting my hand, I caress his cheek with my thumb. He jerks from the touch, his eyes finally meeting mine.

"Jax?" I ask softly.

His eyes flick over my face as if he's searching for something, and his voice is rough as he says, "He loves you."

It wasn't a question, more of an observation. But I answer anyway, "Yes."

"And... you love him."

Again, not a question, but I answer all the same. "Yes."

"Do you love me?" he asks. The way he phrased the question almost sounds desperate.

I'm not sure I want to reveal my answer without first knowing how he feels. I lick my lips, and his eyes follow the movement. "Do you... do you love me?"

His fists unclench as he reaches up to cup my face. "My little wolf, you have dug your claws and teeth into me so deep, I fear it to be fatal. My heart bleeds for you, and I wish for it to never end."

"Jax..." His eyes follow his thumb as it brushes over my bottom lip.

"Do I love you?" I gasp when his eyes meet mine again. His eyes gleam as his voice trembles. "Yes. I love you. Desperately so."

My voice is quieter than I mean for it to be as I say, "I love you, Jax."

Jax's lips are suddenly on mine. I was expecting it to be hungry and desperate, but instead, he's soft and slow as he kisses me. My hands come up to hold his wrist while he holds my face.

I pull away first, a bit breathless. My eyes must look glazed because Jax smirks, his thumb caressing my lip again as he pleads, "Say it again."

I smile as I repeat, "I love you."

He groans and kisses me, then pulls away with a huff. "Not going to lie, I'm going to be needy for a while. I love hearing you say that."

I laugh as I tease, "Well, can you be needy on the bed? My knees are starting to hurt."

He smiles as he stands, helping me up and making our way over to the bed where Luka sits. I'm, of course, in the middle as we pile on and snuggle together. I let out a hum of contentment as I'm surrounded by their warmth.

My thoughts drift to Silas as I realize that I haven't spent as much time with him as I would like. He's been really busy, though. He mentioned that Marvin was creating issues in the skin districts. I groan at the thought of Marvin.

Jax hums behind me. "What's wrong, Sweets?"

"Nothing. I was just thinking."

"Thinking about what?" Luka asks.

Debating if I should talk to them about Silas or not, I finally cave. They are brothers, and if this odd relationship is going to work, it's going to rely on open communication. "I was thinking that I haven't been able to spend much time with Silas due to him being so busy. Which then lead to me thinking about Marvin, since he's the reason Silas is so busy."

Both Jax and Luka growl at the name, then Jax huffs out a sigh. "That fucker has been difficult lately."

"It's my fault he's causing so many issues for you guys."

Luka snorts. "He's been an issue for a while. The only difference is we can do something about it now since he's breaking rules."

"Still."

"No, no more thoughts about that fucker. Fuck him!" Jax grunts out.

"Fine, Fine. Anyway, I haven't been able to spend much time with Silas. He's usually shut up in his office working. I've gone up there a few times to find him asleep at his desk."

Luka hums. "We should offer to help him out a bit. You should be able to spend some time with him, too, if you want."

"I do," I whisper.

Jax groans. "I fucking hate this side of shit."

"Marvin is technically your domain. I don't understand why Silas is dealing with him anyway," Luka points out helpfully.

Jax shrugs. "I threatened to kill him on sight if I see him."

"Jax," Luka reprimands.

"What? It's not my fault the man has a killable face."

I laugh and can't help but ask, "Killable face?"

"Yeah, you know. A face that's just so killable, you can't help but want to stab it."

I snicker. "No wonder Silas won't let you near him."

Jax groans again. "Yeah. Well, I suppose I should offer to take on more of the workload." He snuggles closer as he says, "Tomorrow. Right now, I want all the Macy time I can get."

I laugh as Luka hums his agreement. "Boys! It's only afternoon."

"Re-charge time," Luka mumbles.

Rolling my eyes, I say, "Too early for naps. Come on, we have things to do."

"Nothing more important than snuggling with you right now," Jax murmurs into my back.

I can't really argue. "Fine. But let me at least set an alarm."

"Nope," they say in unison.

These two have me snuggled in so tight that trying to get free would be futile. Seems Silas is going to have to be our alarm if anything urgent happens. Their breathing slows down sooner than I expected as they both begin to snore quietly. I smile as I stare up at the ceiling. They love me. Truly love me.

I find my thoughts drifting to Silas again, and I can't help the heartache I feel weighing on my chest. I've missed him. Do I love him too? I mean, I cared about him before the incident, and after the incident, he opened up to me. He's kept his promise about not hiding away. He spends as much time with me as he can, but work has been keeping us apart. My chest warms the more I think about him. I love him... but do I want to share that with him yet?

CHAPTER THIRTY-ONE
SILAS

My head is currently resting in Macy's lap as we sit on the couch watching TV. Jax and Luka went out for the night, doing some Underground work. Which I thought was odd. But they insisted they take on some of the work I need to get done because I've been spending too much time in the office and not enough time with Macy. I couldn't argue because it's true.

Macy asked me to sit with her, and to be honest, I didn't want to say no. I sat down beside her, and she laughed.

"What?"

She pats her lap. "I can tell you're tired. You have dark circles under your eyes. Lay down."

I've been falling asleep in my office more often than my bed. I arch a brow. "You sure?"

She nods with a soft smile. "If you fall asleep it's okay. I just want you to be with me. Jax and Luka usually snuggle with me, plus this place is too quiet when you guys aren't here."

I hum in reply. We have been gone a lot the last few days, and she had turned down the offer to come with us. I slowly lower my head into her lap, not really sure what to do after that. No one has ever done this with me before, not that I would trust anyone else enough. She slips her fingers through my hair, playing with the long strands. I shiver as her thumb caresses the short hairs on the side of my head. My body slowly begins to relax at her touch, sinking deeper into the couch.

I lie there for a few minutes just watching the screen but not really seeing anything. I'm stuck in my head. Macy has a better relationship with my brothers; I've seen the way she looks at them. Does she look at me like that? I've heard her say I love you to them a few times now. Does she love me too?

I huff out a sigh. Why the hell would she love me? I treated her like shit. I handed her back to Marvin. Sharing a brief heart-to-heart with her doesn't change any of that.

Her fingers are still playing with my hair as she asks, "What's wrong?"

"Nothing," I whisper. This is stupid, why does it matter? I should be thankful for whatever she gives me now. I should be thankful she can stand to be around me at all. She should despise me for what I did to her, but I've never once seen hatred in her eyes when she looked at me.

"Silas? Tell me what's wrong."

I shift so I'm looking up at her. Her gaze feels intense as she stares down at me, concern shining in her eyes. Fuck it, why not. I may as well find out if there's a chance, however small, that she could love me. Just fucking ask her! Trying not to lose my courage I say, "Look into my eyes and say... I love you." What. The. Fuck. Silas? What are you doing? I don't even know why I'm doing this. This is a terrible fucking idea!

Her eyes widen, and she hesitates for a moment before she says, "I love you."

Does she mean it? Should I test it a bit more? What if I make it sound like I don't believe her? I arch a brow as I say, "Okay... I'm not believing that at this point, so say it again." Why the fuck am I so desperate for this? Why are you testing this miniscule relationship you have with her?

Her eyes soften as she slides her fingers through my hair. "I love you."

My heart stops for a moment. That... that sounded like she meant it. I search her eyes before whispering, "Again."

She smiles softly as her other hand comes up to cup my cheek. "I love you," she whispers.

My chest begins to ache because I want to believe her. "Again."

She doesn't falter. Her eyes never leave mine as she repeats, "I love you."

My throat grows thick as my chest constricts. I force the word out, "Again."

She leans down, pressing her lips to mine in a light caress. She pulls back just enough that I can feel her words across my lips. "I love you, Silas."

I close my eyes when I feel them start to burn. Reaching up, I thread my fingers in her hair to keep her close. My voice cracks when I say, "One more time... please."

"I'll say it as many times as you need, Silas. I love you."

I want to say it back. I need to say it back. This beautiful woman who has demolished every wall I've built around me. Glass though they may be, to allow others to look in but never touch. Like an object on display. But she's done it. Macy has fractured my walls and tamed the beast.

An animal built for blood and violence. To do my job and do it well has fallen to her charm and sweet touches. I've tried to stop myself from falling, but it was no use.

She's now a chink in my well-worn armor. A chink that will lead me to ruin. If my enemies find her. If they take her. I will lay waste to the Underground for her. For her... I will do anything.

Anything... to watch her rosy lips form those three words. To hear her say them just one more time. My eyes meet hers again, and I feel the tears fall as I whisper, "One more time."

She presses a soft kiss to my lips again, as I feel the words echo in my long forgotten soul. "I love you, Silas."

I've only broken for one other person in my life, but nothing compares to the way I shatter for her now.

Macy

I hadn't planned on telling Silas I loved him. I wasn't even sure if I did truly love him or if my feelings for the others were getting muddled with my feelings for him. But the moment he looked up at me with those desperate eyes and demanded I say those words, I couldn't deny it any longer.

I love him. I love all three of them more than I ever thought possible. They have become my safe place. My home. As I repeated myself over and over, my eyes never wavered from his. And that's when I realized something.

Silas's eyes were becoming my favorite thing about him. He said so much with his eyes. And right now they are pleading and lost. They hold the anguish of a man who has suffered more pain than any one person should ever experience. So agonized, but underneath, so full of hope that he's afraid to feel. Hope that I would tell him I loved him too.

But his eyes also remind me of my favorite season. Late autumn, when the leaves change from green to a deep brown. They are hazel, yes, but swirled with green and browns. The warmth I feel when I look into his eyes and watch as they soften for me. Only me.

It was as if they swirled in a storm of rain and wind, to cease only when he looked at me. When his eyes met mine, the anger and torment disappeared. He looked up at me, pleading with me to say those words over and over again. I thought he would get tired of asking, but he never did. It was as if each time I repeated the words, a piece of his soul knitted back together. The darkness clouding his eyes lifted with each repetition.

He didn't tire of asking, but the exhaustion from weeks of sleeping in his office did eventually catch up to him. His eyes slowly drifted closed each time he asked me to repeat myself. His voice got quieter and softer as he slowly drifted off to sleep. Letting out a content sigh, I caress the frown line building between his brows. He hums in his sleep as he snuggles closer, and I smile.

I've never seen him sleep this soundly before. Although, to be honest, I've never seen the man sleep. But Jax and Luka have mentioned that he has trouble sleeping multiple times. My fingers play with his hair as he snores softly while the TV continues to shine in the background. Now silent so as to not disturb him.

I don't want anything to wake him from his slumber. Not now that he has finally found a moment of peace.

CHAPTER THIRTY-TWO
MACY

I've been back a few days, and I haven't been this happy in a long time. Jax and Luka have done nothing but spoil me, even though I told them not to. They said they felt like they needed to make up for what they had done even after I forgave them. Silas, though, has made the biggest change. I'm not sure if it's because I told him I loved him or that he was trying to make up for betraying me. Maybe it was a bit of both.

He purposefully seeks me out throughout the day now. If I am in the kitchen eating he will come up behind me and wrap his arms around me for a few moments. He will press a kiss to my head before walking away with a soft smile on his face. It surprises me how easily he shows physical affection now. I thought physical touch with him would be the hardest considering our conversation several weeks ago.

These days, he makes sure to finish his paperwork and Underground tasks so he can sneak into my bedroom. He's always trying to beat his brothers to my room so he can pull me close to his chest and savor the few moments together. In those shared moments between the two of us, Silas never talks, and I don't mind. His silence speaks louder than any words.

Currently, we are all in the office discussing a problem within the Underground. Specifically, Jax's territory. The escorts and prostitutes. The problem you may ask? The only man who seems to cause the vein at Silas's temple to pulse; Marvin.

I'm sitting on the corner of Silas's desk as per his request. He said it helps him stay calm. The thought makes me laugh. It couldn't possibly have anything to do with the booty shorts and tank top I am wearing. The vein in his temple continues to pulse as I say, "Si, you need to calm down."

He huffs out a sigh. "It's hard to stay calm when that damn man is a thorn in my side. He has been undermining not only my authority, but Hades' and Persephone's as well."

"He needs to remember who is at the top of the food chain," Jax says as he lounges farther back in his chair.

"And how should we go about reminding him?" Silas growls out, his fingers white-knuckling the arms of the chair.

Hopping off the desk, I plop down into his lap. He grunts as he situates me before wrapping his arms around my waist, pulling me close. He buries his face into my neck, taking a deep breath. I can feel the tension leave his body with each breath as he slowly relaxes.

My fingers caress his forearm, running them up and down. "Better?"

"Yes," he mumbles against my neck.

"Well, this is a bit unfair. Where is my love?" Jax asks with a smirk.

I give him a wink as I say, "I'll give you a little extra love later, how about that?"

"What about me?" Luka asks from the chair beside Jax.

Rolling my eyes, I say, "How about we have a cuddle puddle and everyone gets love."

Silas growls into my neck. "We need to finish this meeting."

"You're the one with our girl in your lap getting distracted," Jax points out with an eye roll of his own.

Silas huffs out a sigh before pulling away to look at his brothers. "As I was saying, how are we going to teach Marvin a lesson?"

Jax runs a frustrated hand down his face. "It would be so much easier if he were a nobody. But he currently runs most of the escort and prostitution rings. If he were a nobody we could easily put someone else in charge. At the moment, too many people use him directly for services."

Luka hums before pointing out, "He isn't paying the escorts and prostitutes the way he should, either. Since he lost Macy, he's been taking it out on the other girls."

I stiffen in Silas's lap, and his grip tightens. "This isn't your fault. We are going to take care of the situation, so don't worry about them."

Jax huffs out a sigh before saying, "We also have another issue. I didn't want to bring it up because escorts and prostitutes in our care disappear all the time." He sees my eyes widen, and he hurries to explain. "I use the word disappear loosely. We know where they go. They usually run off with clients or leave when they have saved up enough money. It's a common thing, especially with those under Marvin's care."

"Then what is the issue?" I ask hesitantly.

"The escorts are the only one's going missing, and they are not notifying me beforehand of where they are going. I find the timing a little too convenient with everything going on with Marvin right now that his highest paying escorts, aside from Macy, are missing."

Panic begins to build inside me. "What do you think he's doing to them?"

His eyes meet mine, filled with apologies he isn't able to voice right now. "My guess is that he is selling them to clients. He doesn't have the connections to sell humans on a wide scale, but he would be able to sell to local clients who prefer a certain type of escort."

Silas presses a kiss to my temple. "Don't worry, little wolf. We are going to stop him. I promise."

I smile at the nickname. "I wish you would call me your moon again."

I feel his smile against my temple. "I cannot deny you, dear." His lips brush next to my ear as he whispers, "Do you trust us, my moon?"

"Yes," I answer without hesitation.

"Then believe me when I say that we will find them and stop him. No one else will be hurt by him again under our watchful eyes."

I nod as I snuggle into his chest. He holds me close as they continue planning. His chest rumbles as he speaks, which seems to soothe some of my worry and panic. My eyes close as his warmth and dark scent surround me. With each breath I take, I feel my body relax. My buzzing mind calms, and I slip farther into the darkness around me.

The last words I hear are, "Rest, my moon."

CHAPTER THIRTY-THREE
MACY

"Alright boys! You promised me shopping!" I jump up from the kitchen table when I see them step out of the elevator. They were down in the gym for their morning workouts while I waited oh-so-patiently for them to finish. Normally, I would be downstairs watching or reading, but they had promised to take me shopping after they were done working out. So I made sure I ate breakfast early, that way I would be ready to go when they were done.

Jax groans as he makes his way to the kitchen and grabs a shaker bottle for his post-workout drink. "Can we take a shower before we leave, Mace? We smell like a dirty locker room."

Silas snorts a laugh as he presses a kiss to my head before joining Jax. "Speak for yourself, brother."

Luka pulls out a chair and sits down beside me. "We smell like sweat, not a locker room. If you smell like a locker room, you should probably get that checked out, brother."

Jax takes a deep gulp of his drink before saying, "I'm taking a shower." He points to Silas then Luka. "If you two want to walk around with sweaty balls, then by all means, don't shower."

Walking around the island, he kisses my forehead saying softly, "Love you, beautiful."

Smiling, I whisper back, "Love you too."

He pulls away with a smile. "I'll be quick, then off to the bookstore."

I nod as I turn to the others. I see the sour looks on their faces as they debate whether to take a shower or not. Rolling my eyes, I say, "Go take a shower. Sweaty balls are gross."

Luka laughs as he leans to kiss my cheek. "Noted. Love you, Mac."

I laugh as I mumble, "Love you."

He smiles as he grabs the shaker cup Silas offers before heading to his room to shower.

My eyes follow his retreat until he disappears up the stairs. I turn to find Silas watching me with pinched brows. I arch a brow in question. "What?"

He shakes his head before gulping down the last of his drink. Still confused, I ask again softly, "What is it, Si?"

Setting the cup down, he leans against the island. His eyes rove over my face before they soften as his gaze meets mine. He opens his mouth before snapping it closed. Huffing out a sigh, he whispers, "You... you know I care for you, right?"

"Of course, I do," I say without hesitation.

His brows furrow as his fingers curl into fists. His eyes flick down to the island. "Just because... just because I don't say..."

I jump up from my spot, making my way around the island to wrap my arms around him. My chest presses hard against his back as I hold him tight. "It's okay. It's okay, I don't need the words. I don't need to hear it so long as you keep showing me. Your actions speak louder than anything you could say."

He moves his hands to cover mine, pressing them harder into his stomach. His voice is rough as he whispers, "You're too good to me."

I laugh against his back. "And you spoil me. So I suppose we are even."

He huffs. "I suppose I should go take a shower, so we can get you more books."

I loosen my grip around him enough to shimmy myself between him and the island. He looks down at me with a smile. "What are you doing, Macy?"

I smile up at him as I raise on tiptoes to press a kiss to his lips. My lips hover over his as I say, "I love you."

His gaze softens as he presses a soft kiss against my lips. Pulling away, he caresses my cheek with his thumb as his eyes rake over my face. His voice is quiet as he says, "My beautiful moon."

I hum in contentment. "Your moon."

"Such a distraction you are," he says with a laugh. "I should really go take a shower."

Laughing, I nod, pulling away. "Go take your shower. I want new books!"

Smirking, he presses a quick kiss to my forehead before pulling away completely to head upstairs. I watch him walk away with a smile on my face.

"Mace! I cannot possibly hold any more!" Jax huffs from behind the pile I managed to stack in his arms.

"Good thing I have three boyfriends." I turn to Luka, holding out another book.

Taking it from my grip, he says, "You realize we will have to carry these all to the car, right?"

I hum as I continue looking over the bookshelf. "Good thing my three boyfriends are all strong and capable of carrying so many heavy things."

"Two boyfriends who are capable of carrying the books, Macy," Silas states matter of factly.

I arch a brow in question. "Two boyfriends?"

He points to himself as he says, "This boyfriend has to stay book free in case there's trouble."

He does have a point. Nodding, I continue browsing the shelves. "You're right."

He chuckles as he keeps an eye on our surroundings. "I often am."

"Debatable," I say absentmindedly, pulling out several more books and handing them to Luka. After about three hours, I realized that I couldn't possibly get anymore. Jax's and Luka's arms are filled with books not including the ones I'm holding.

As we approach the register, the cashier's eyes widen. I set down my haul while Jax and Luka stand behind me, arms full. "You... you want all of those books?"

I nod with a grin. "Yes, please."

She holds a walkie talkie to her mouth as she says, "Could I have some help at check out?" A confirmation comes through immediately, and she points to the register beside her. "If you would like to set those books down over there, I'll have another person come up and help."

Jax and Luka both set the books down as she looks back to me. "Will this all be together?"

I feel Silas step up behind me as he says, "All together. I can pay for them separately."

She nods, seemingly nervous with Silas watching her. I laugh as her eyes bounce between each guy while she rings up the books. The cashier beside her starts doing the same. They ring up the last of the purchases, handing the bags over to Jax and Luka.

"We'll go ahead and take these to the car in case you want to do any other shopping," Jax says as he presses a kiss to my forehead.

Luka does the same as he says, "Grab yourself a coffee too."

I clap my hands happily. "I do love coffee."

He smirks. "I know. We'll be right back."

I should have known that Marvin would never just let me be. I should have known that going to the bookstore would give him the opening he needed. I was no longer safe in the wolf's den. I was out in the open.

Silas

I watch Macy happily hum while sipping her coffee, my hand firmly in her grasp as she swings my arm and bops to the beat in her head. I'm not a touchy feely person, but when it comes to her, I want her touch. No, I need her touch. I crave it.

"What are you humming, love?"

Her eyes flick to mine as she shrugs. "Nothing really. Just a random beat, I suppose."

We are outside the bookstore waiting for Jax and Luka to return from dropping her books off at the car. Twisting my wrist enough to look at my watch, I frown when I notice it's been about ten minutes. I look around, but I don't see them anywhere. They should have been back by now.

As if echoing my thoughts Macy says, "They should have made it back already."

I don't like this, and I'm getting a bad feeling. My brothers and I are strong on our own, but with everything going on right now, we are stronger together. Looking around again to make sure we're not being watched, I tug on Macy's hand. "Let's head to the car."

Her brows knit together, but she doesn't argue as she nods, following my lead. We are getting close to the parking garage when I hear a loud pop. I stop, looking around as I push Macy behind me.

Several more quick pops follow, and suddenly we are engulfed in smoke. Fuck! My grip on Macy tightens as I try to see through the smoke. It's no use though. I can feel the panic building in my chest because I know what this is. My head explodes with pain as I fall forward, and Macy is ripped out of my hand.

She screams as I try to clear my head. "Macy!" I yell, trying to get my bearings as I wave my arms around me, trying to dissipate the smoke. Her screams disappear, and I'm greeted only by silence.

The smoke is starting to irritate my throat, and I start to hyperventilate. My vision is still blurry as I try to blink away the pain. "Macy!" I scream, but I'm greeted by nothing but silence. My phone rings, and I reach for it quickly, picking it up. "Hello?"

"Seems you've lost your whore, boss man. Your brothers are stuffed in the trunk of your car, by the way."

"Marvin," I growl. "Where the fuck is Macy?"

He tuts. "Now, now, that's no way to speak to the man who holds the well being of your woman in his hands."

I know where this is going. "What do you want, Marvin?"

"What every man wants in my position, Silas," he hisses my name as if it's the plague.

"Pussy?"

"Hum… close. That is a very important P when it comes to my position, but what I want is power."

"You have power," I growl.

"Yes. Well, you took my highest-paying escort. She's also the best pussy I've had in years. But I'm willing to part with her, for a price."

"What do you want?" I yell. My patience is growing thin as I try to make my way toward the parking garage to help my brothers.

"I want a meeting."

"With who?"

"Hades."

I let out a dry laugh. "You want a meeting with Hades? The fuck you expect me to get you a meeting with Hades for?"

He hums as he says, "Not sure. Don't care, either. If you want your woman back, get me that meeting."

I already know what Jace would say because Jane would threaten his balls if he didn't agree. Though, I doubt Marvin would get as far as the cave entrance before Jace had the Hellhounds devour this douchebag. "I'll get you the meeting. You know where the Underworld compound is?"

"Everyone in the Underground knows where the compound is."

I finally get to the car when I ground out, "Be there tomorrow night." I don't even bother to listen for his reply; I hang up. Shoving my phone into my back pocket, I press the key fob button to open the trunk.

There, lying in a heap, are my brothers. Passed out cold. Seems Marvin had back up. They must have managed to gas my brothers so they didn't have to fight them. Smart on their part. Jax alone would have beat them to a pulp.

I turn to lean up against the bumper of the car as I send Jace a text. I never thought I'd have to send this text again. Just because I was no longer the Alpha of his Hellhounds doesn't mean I had forgotten every code we had.

Hades: The Gods kill at your command.

His reply is almost immediate, and in code as well, which makes me let out a sigh of relief. Everyone will be there, including the Hellhounds. They will be ready to spill blood if necessary to get our girl back. *Stay strong. Your wolves are coming for you, My Goddess.*

CHAPTER THIRTY-FOUR
SILAS

We arrive at the designated spot where we told Marvin we would be waiting. I don't think he expects the whole Underworld crew to be waiting for him outside the cave for him, though. I'm not sure what this fucker is planning, but all I know is that we are going to get our girl back. By whatever means necessary.

Jace stands at the mouth of the cave where the doors lead inside. He gives me a nod in greeting. Jane stands beside him. I arch a brow in her direction. "Shouldn't you be at home considering?" I wave a hand in the general direction of her belly.

She looks down at her belly, which has rapidly grown over the last few months, then back up at me. "Do you think I'm incapable of fighting just because I'm growing a human, Alpha?"

Smirking, I say, "I would never doubt your ability to fight, Seph. Only thought the guys would lock you up considering what could happen."

"I believe she would castrate us if we dared," Zane says as he groans from beside her.

I nod in agreement. I have no doubt that she would. When I hear a car roaring in the distance, I turn. The others are closing in to ensure we are well protected.

"Hellhounds, get ready. There's a car approaching. I want eyes on our surroundings as well as on that car," Jace calls out before readying himself for the inevitable fight.

We all wait as the car parks a good distance away, and other cars slowly follow suit. A familiar figure steps out of the backseat, flanking the single car. I ready my gun to end this all right now, but I stop when I see the smile on his face as he tuts. "I wouldn't do that if I were you."

I hear grunting as he pulls someone out behind him. My eyes widen as I watch Marvin hold a knife to my girl's neck. No our girl. She belongs to my brothers and I. I knew we should have handled this fucking creep when it seemed like he was obsessed with our girl. This whole meeting was a trap; I knew that, but we figured a meet-up at the Underworld cave would deter anyone from doing anything stupid. I gave Marvin too much credit.

I look next to me to find my brothers hardly daring to move. My eyes roam the grounds in search of the Hellhounds who have the area surrounded but refuse to move unless ordered. Hades is holding out a hand to still the restless Hounds until he sees an opening. Seph is holding her daggers at her side, waiting as well, but I can see that she's trying to find a way to save her best friend. The others are waiting behind Hades and Seph for orders.

I look back to Macy, grinding my teeth in frustration. How are we going to get her out of his grasp? I watch as he presses the knife hard into her neck, and I can't stop the scream that tears from my throat, "Selene!"

Marvin chuckles as his hold on her hair tightens, and he says, "Seems you got a new pet name, little doll. Do you like your new owners? You must be fucking them real nice for them to name you after a goddess."

I can't stop myself from running toward them. "Selene," I scream again. My throat is raw from the force of it. She is our Selene. Our guiding light. The moon we howl at as we bath in her light. Our goddess. The beast inside of me roars. The beast born and bred from all the emotions I've been holding back for so long. It was raw and destructive. And it wanted out.

Kill. KILL. KILL!

Mine. MINE. MINE!

Time seems to slow as I run toward them, and I watch Marvin's smile widen. He throws away the knife, reaching behind him and pulling out a taser. He presses it against her chest, and with a dark laugh he says, "If I can't have her, no one can."

My eyes widen as he hits the button, and I watch in horror as Macy's eyes widen. Her mouth gapes open in a soundless scream as her eyes roll back. He throws her to the ground before turning to run away like the coward he is. I hear Hades scream for the Hounds to attack, but I'm not paying them any mind.

My eyes are on Macy as she crumples to the ground in a heap. My knees slam the grass as I drop down beside her. I flip her over, running my hands up her chest to find the burn from where Marvin held the taser. I press my hand harder against her chest when I notice it's not rising. I hold my breath, waiting for her next breath, but there's nothing. She's not breathing. I move my hand to her neck to feel for a pulse in case my hands were shaking too much. But I was right. There's no steady beat. Nothing.

My own heart races as I move over her, placing my shaking hands in the correct position on her sternum to start CPR. I hear my brothers run up behind me.

"What's wrong?!" Jax yells.

"She doesn't have a pulse," I grunt out, as I keep track of the count and beat for each chest compression.

Jax doesn't say anything else as he bends down, watching each forceful press to her chest until I get to thirty. He gently elevates her chin to the correct position before giving her two rescue breaths. I begin again, and I hear Luka yell, "I'm calling the doctor now!"

I nod as I continue CPR. I'm huffing as I say, "You can't leave now. Not now, Macy." I'm trying to control my breathing as my brother and I continue trying to revive her. I can feel the tears burning behind my eyes as we keep going with no change in her vitals. "You said you loved me, right?" I choke out.

It's getting harder to breathe as my throat grows tight with emotion. I'm gulping down air with the effort it's taking to continue making sure her heart beats on top of keeping a lid on my overflowing emotions. "I didn't say it back," I grit out. I can't see anything at this angle. Everything is becoming blurry in front of me as I fight to keep this woman with us. "You have to come back, so I can say it. But you know, don't you? You know how I feel. That's why you're making me work for it."

I hear a thump, and I look up to find Jax punching the ground beside him as he watches us work. My vision is just clear enough now that I can see the tears streaming down his face as he says, "Thirty." Then he lowers to press his lips to hers, giving her two more breaths.

I begin my compressions again and hear him say, "The prince is supposed to wake his princess with a kiss, remember, Mace?" He snorts out a watery laugh as he continues, "I know we aren't much as far as princely males go but—" He chokes on a sob as he lowers to press his forehead against hers. "We will treat you like the goddess you are. So please come back to us," he begs.

I hear Luka scream, "The doctor is here!"

I continue chest compressions as the doctor drops down and slides up next to me. "What happened?" he asks as he pulls stuff out of his bag.

I clear my throat and say, "She was shocked by a taser."

"How long have you been doing this?"

I shake my head. "I'm not sure. I haven't really been keeping track of time."

Seph yells, "He's been doing CPR for about six minutes now. It's a good thing you were so close, Doc."

He nods as he pulls out a box with little electrodes attached to it. He moves closer, working around me as he rips open the rest of her shirt. He places the pads in specific locations and then turns to grab a bag with a mask attached to it. He passes the bag to Jax as he turns on the box.

"What's that?" Luka asks.

Without looking away from Macy he says, "It's an AED. It's a defibrillator; it will provide a shock to her heart. I'm hoping we can shock her heart back into a steady rhythm." He turns around yelling, "Get the medical bay ready! I'll need to monitor her for a while."

A woman yells back, "Right away, Doctor!"

He turns back around and sighs, "Alright, little lady, you have some very upset males here waiting for your return. I've been fighting for souls my whole life, and you better believe I will fight just as hard for yours."

He turns to me and says, "When I say clear, I need you to stop compressions. Nobody touch her. I will shock her, and if I don't get a heartbeat, I will tell you when to start again. You do not stop until I say clear again, understood?"

I nod as he turns to Jax. "I am going to try to time this perfectly. Once Silas says thirty, you will give two breaths, and then I will say clear. We will do this cycle every time the AED needs to charge, understood?"

He nods as the doctor turns back to me. "Where are you at?"

"Twenty-five," I grunt out.

He nods, pointing to Jax. "Get ready."

The moment I say thirty, Jax gives Macy two breaths. "Clear," the doc calls out, and Jax and I both lift our hands, showing that we are no longer touching her. He presses the button, and I watch as Macy's body jolts. We wait a moment before the doctor yells, "Start again."

Without hesitation, I begin compressions again. I know I should probably switch out with someone, but I won't stop till her heart beats again. The doctor nods, looking between us once more. He waits for Jax to give two breaths before saying, "Clear."

I wait for his directions as he watches the AED. He opens his mouth and says, "Star—wait!" He pulls out a stethoscope, pressing it to her chest. "We have a pulse!" he yells and gestures for someone. "Get her to the med unit, now! We need to get her on the vent. She's not breathing on her own just yet."

I collapse on the ground, my arms exhausted, as I watch several nurses surround Macy and lift her onto a gurney. A nurse takes the bag from Jax and begins giving breaths as they race toward the cave entrance.

I want to follow but I can't. All I can do is choke out, "Macy." It sounds broken, even to my ears, as I watch them wheel her away. I can't move as I lie on the ground. I feel my breathing increase as my heart thumps even harder. We lost her. She died. Macy fucking died!

My forearm covers my eyes as a sob slips between my lips. I squeeze my eyes shut as they start to burn again. I can feel myself beginning to hyperventilate as another sob tears through my chest. The tears slip between my lids and glide into my hair. I feel someone lie down beside me and take my empty hand. I squeeze my brother's fingers, knowing it's Jax. He slides in closer to me so our shoulders brush.

I can feel his shoulders shaking as he tries to hold back sobs of his own. His breathing is choppy as he squeezes my hand tighter. Another body settles on my opposite side, and when I feel fingers slide into my belt loop, I know it's Luka. He's always been the one to hold this family together. He's always been comfortable being open with his feelings and emotions. So it comes to no surprise when his head settles down next to mine. I can hear him sucking in breaths when he can as he openly sobs.

At hearing our baby brother cry, Jax can no longer hold back. He lets out a gut-wrenching sob of his own as he gets swept up in the grief and despair of this moment. I bite my lip, hard, trying to keep the growing sob in my chest at bay. I need to be strong for my brothers. The steady rock they lean on. But the longer I hear their cries, the more my beast whimpers in pain. No longer able to hold everything in, I let out a bellowing cry. The ache in my chest feels like I'm being shredded to pieces as I continue to roar.

Our wolves howl as our moon no longer shines down upon us. The need to bathe in her light is so crippling. All we can do is howl at the sky as we beg for our moon goddess to come back to us.

CHAPTER THIRTY-FIVE
MACY

They say when you die your life flashes before your eyes. Childhood all the way up to your current life, supposedly playing across your eyelids like a movie. Well, I'm here to tell you, that's horse shit. Or, maybe my life sucked so badly that nothing worth remembering came into view?

What I do see are flashes of the men who've made me feel so loved and cherished. My wolves.

Luka's smiling face flashes across the darkness in front of me. He always knows how to make me laugh and feel wanted. Cherished. I have to admit, I fell hard for him.

A picture of Jax smirking flashes next. My playful man. Never a dull moment with him around. I've never met a man who wanted cuddles as much as him. Always needing that touch to know I'm there.

Somber eyes flash across my vision next. Silas. My heart broke the day he asked me to tell him I loved him. As if he thought it impossible for someone to love him at all. I could see he wanted to say it back but held his tongue. That didn't bother me, I know he's a man of action more than words. He shows me he loves me in so many ways.

Suddenly, my body jolts in the darkness. It feels like a zap throughout my body. Like a static shock but more powerful. And more painful.

Pain blooms in my chest, and I rub at it with hands I didn't realize I had. Where the fuck am I? I look around, but I'm still surrounded by darkness.

My body jolts again, and it feels as if I'm falling. I scream as pain sears across my chest while I fall. I don't know what the hell is happening, but it feels like my body slams into something. I begin to panic when I realize I have absolutely no control over my body. It's as if I'm trapped in a cage.

I can hear people yelling around me as I feel a puff of air inflate my lungs. Fucking hell! What's happening?

I feel like I'm floating on air when I barely hear it, my name. I heard it though; I know I did. I heard him. Silas. He sounds so heartbroken.

What could break my strong and silent man? Luka's words from what feels like a lifetime ago return.

You are his chink.

Me? I broke him?

CHAPTER THIRTY-SIX

SILAS

It's been a week since the confrontation with Marvin. My brothers and I have refused to leave the medical unit at the cave since the day Macy died on us. The doctor says that she's doing much better. She had a few arrhythmias at the very beginning, but her heart has since stabilized, and she's been off the vent for a few days. She hasn't woken up yet, and the doctor says that it's normal after a trauma like this. We won't know how much damage has been done to her brain until she wakes up.

I don't care if there's anything wrong with her. I don't care if she's completely forgotten us. It will tear my heart apart if she doesn't remember us; if she doesn't love us. Her moonlight will have dimmed, but if I can just bathe in its light, if only for a moment, I'll hold onto it forever. I'll hold onto that feeling for the rest of my life. I just want her to wake up.

With each beat of my heart, I will shatter without her. Slowly hemorrhaging with each beat, but I will gladly die just to see her hazel-green eyes one more time. Her eyes... I need to see her eyes. She would joke and laugh while I stared at her. *My eyes are nothing special. They are a common color.*

I disagree. Her eyes are jade and amber combined; the brightest of jewels when she laughs or smiles. They may seem common to her, but I have seen thousands of eyes. None have shined as brightly as hers.

Sunshine and laughter are common as well, but that doesn't make them any less beautiful. She is the sunshine peeking through my storm. Her eyes are the beacon leading me back to her. Leading me home.

I need her to lead me home. My mind is filled with nothing but darkness and chaos. Even with my brothers around, I feel lonely. I want to go home. I need to feel at home again.

So I wait for her eyes to open and to hear the rasp of her voice calling my name. I rub at the ache resting heavy in my chest as I watch the monitor. I watch each beat of her heart along with each breath she takes.

Jax bumps my shoulder, and I mumble, "Yeah?"

"Have you eaten?" he asks in a rough voice.

I shake my head, refusing to take my eyes off the monitor. "No," I answer gruffly. I haven't spoken much in the past week. With the constant ache in my chest, I've been afraid that if I open my mouth a sob would sneak its way out. I've never thought of myself as a man who showed emotion, let alone a man who cried. But this woman has me in a choke hold. If she leaves this world, I can't guarantee I wouldn't follow behind. Not physically. I could never leave my brothers, but my heart would die along with her. Although, I feel my brothers would be the same. A pack of heartless wolves in charge of the Underground wouldn't go well for the people of this territory.

Jax places a hand on my shoulder, giving it a squeeze. "You need to eat."

I shake my head again. "Not until I know she's okay."

Jax sighs and says, "Please eat. You can change and take a shower too. Jane went to the house and picked up some of our stuff."

I tear my gaze from the monitor to look up at my brother. He has dark circles under his eyes, and he looks like he's taken a shower, but it doesn't seem to have refreshed him. He looks just as exhausted as I feel. None of us have really slept for fear of something happening if we closed our eyes. He lowers himself to rest his forehead against mine as he whispers, "I'll watch over her. You will only be a few steps away. Take a quick shower and then eat. Please."

I close my eyes for a moment before nodding. I can't say no to my brother when he's like this. My brothers have always been my weakness. "Okay," I whisper. I look back at the monitor, seeing that there has been no change. Sighing, I stand from the chair, heading toward the shower right on the other side of the wall. I strip as I make my way into the bathroom, taking as quick of a shower as I can. Stepping back out, I pull on the fresh clothes, feeling a little bit better now that I am clean.

Stepping back into Macy's room, I see Jax has moved the chair up next to the bed. I hear him snoring softly as his head rests on the edge of her bed. I look to the other side and find Luka in a similar position, his hair tousled and wet from his shower. So much for guard dogs. I walk closer to find that they are each holding one of her hands. I can't stop the tilt to my lips as I see my two youngest brothers finally getting some much needed rest.

Tearing my eyes from them, I look around the room to find a sandwich sitting on a chair in the far corner. I walk over, grabbing the sandwich and the chair. I pull the chair to sit right in front of Macy's bed. Dropping into the seat, I take a bite of the sandwich as I watch her vitals on the screen. My stomach growls in pain as I continue eating. I probably shouldn't have gone so long without food.

I can feel my eyes growing heavy, and I try to fight it. I can't sleep yet. Not... yet. The steady beeping of the heart monitor changes for a moment, increasing its speed before slowing back down. My head jerks up to the screen to see if there are any issues with her other vitals.

I huff out a sigh as my gaze returns to her, and I freeze. Green hazel eyes are staring back at me. I don't dare move in case this is a dream. Maybe I fell asleep without realizing it. I was tired enough. My chest begins to ache as I hold my breath, too afraid any sudden movement will have me opening my eyes to find hers still closed. My chest wouldn't ache if this were a dream, right?

I slowly stand from my chair as I let out a puff of air. I move quietly so as not to wake my brothers. Her eyes follow me as I stop at the end of the bed. She looks to her left, then her right before her eyes meet mine again. My chest explodes when her soft voice rasps, "Hey, Silas."

I can't stop myself as I blurt out in a loud whisper, "I love you!"

Her eyes widen for a moment before softening. She smiles as she says, "I love you, too."

I shake my head as I feel my eyes begin to burn. "No. I don't think you understand."

Her brows furrow as she asks softly, "What do you mean?"

I reach forward and grasp her small feet still covered in the blankets. I stare down at them while trying to keep my voice quiet as I say, "I need you like the wolf needs the moon. I want to bathe under your moonlight forever. My soul aches to feel you near, and my heart beats only when you are within my sight. I was a beast who felt nothing and wanted nothing from this world until you. I told you before that I couldn't lose you.

You are the only thing that matters. I cannot lose you. My soul and heart would follow behind. You are the only one who quiets the beast within me. You are the only one who gives me any peace." I choke on the last of my words, no longer able to hold back my emotions. My vision blurs as I look back up at her. Her eyes are wide as I whisper out, "You have broken me in ways I didn't know were possible. But I'll take each crack in my heart that hemorrhages and every shattered piece of my soul to be with you. I will gladly burn at the altar as a sacrifice for you, Moon Goddess, if I could only bathe in your light."

I watch as she slowly slips her hands out of Jax's and Luka's so as not to wake them. Careful of the cords and tubes she is connected to, she shifts onto her knees, crawling slowly toward me as I continue to watch her.

When she's finally in front of me, she reaches out, cupping my face in her hands. She caresses my cheeks with her thumbs. Her soft touch forces my eyes to close as I try to hold back the onslaught of new tears from falling. But they only fall faster.

I suck in a deep breath before whispering, "It's... been so... dark without you."

She pulls me forward to press her lips softly to mine. It's gentle as she pulls away just enough so that her lips caress mine as she says, "I'm here now."

We must not have been quiet enough because a deep voice asks, "Mace?"

She pulls away to look over her shoulder with a smile. "Hey, Jax."

He blinks owlishly a few times before his eyes widen and he jumps up from the chair. He rushes to where I'm standing with her, and the moment he's close enough, he engulfs her and me in a hug. He's gentle with her, but the arm encircling me holds tight as his fingers dig into my shoulder.

"You scared the shit out of us, Mace," he rasps out as he presses his face into her hair. He takes in a few deep breaths before pulling away when he hears Luka's tentative voice, "Mac?"

"Our sunshine brother hasn't been himself without you," Jax says with a sad smile.

Macy turns her head in Luka's direction as she says, "It's hard to believe my sun hasn't been himself. He is Apollo after all."

Luka's eyes shine with tears as he rasps out, "It's been hard to shine without my moon for company."

"The moon can't shine without the sun."

Luka stands, reaching out to cup her cheek as he says, "Then I shall be your sun." He presses a soft kiss to her lips before pulling away. "Our love shall be the envy of gods and goddesses alike."

She smirks as she says, "I like the sound of that."

CHAPTER THIRTY-SEVEN
MACY

The machine behind me starts to beep annoyingly, and I realize that some of the wires attached to me have come loose. I huff out a sigh as I pull out of the guy's arms. Backing up so that I'm now lying back down, I press down on the sticky patch on my abdomen with a wire attached to it. The machine still beeps, so I move to the one on my chest, pressing it back down. The alarming beep quiets as it picks up my steady heartbeat again.

I look back up to find three worried faces. With a smile, I say, "I'm okay."

Jax rolls his eyes. "You are not fine. That bandage on your chest is going to be there for another few weeks due to the severity of the burn. Your neck will at least heal up nicely with minimal scarring. But that bandage will need to stay on for at least a few more days. You are nowhere near being fine."

I huff out a sigh as I nod in agreement. "Fine. What if I said that I'm doing better?"

Luka snorts. "Your expectations are low if you think this..." he gestures to all of me, "is doing better."

I shrug. "My heart is beating, so I'll take it." I take in their worried looks and really stop to look at them. They all have dark circles and red rimmed eyes. They look exhausted. Silas looks the worst, though.

I look around the room and notice there are two empty hospital beds beside mine. I point toward each bed as I say, "You guys look like shit. Pull up those beds next to mine, and get some shut eye."

Silas begins to move toward one of them, but I stop him. "Not you. Jax and Luka can get those. You are sleeping with me."

He gives me an arched brow before looking between his brothers. "I probably shouldn't. I can sleep in one of the chairs."

I groan as I say, "If you don't come over here, I'll just come drag you."

He narrows his eyes on me as he says, "You wouldn't dare."

With a smirk, I begin to shimmy on the bed. The machine starts to alarm the moment the wires connected to me start to loosen.

Silas growls as he rushes to me. "Fine! I'm here."

I smile as I look up at him. "That's what happens when you're stubborn."

He glares at me as he says, "I think that's the pot calling the kettle black."

I grin as I move forward enough for him to slip onto the bed behind me. "Stop acting like you don't want to snuggle with me and climb in. The others are waiting on you."

He lets out a grunt but does as I said. The others move the beds in close once he's up beside me.

I slide backward, and he immediately slips his arms around me, holding me close.

His face lowers into the crook of my neck as he takes in a deep inhale. His grip around me tightens as he whispers, "You don't smell like you."

"Sorry. I wish I could take a shower," I whisper back.

His head shakes a bit before one of his hands slips up to rest between my breasts. Normally, in this sorta situation I would be like, what the hell? I literally almost died, and you want to get handsy. But I notice his hand stops right above my heart. I hear his breath hitch as he says, "Sorry. Can I please feel your heartbeat?"

I cover his hand with mine as I reply, "For as long as you need." I slip my hand from his as Jax and Luka settle closer to me. They each grab onto a wrist, holding them so that they can feel the reassuring beat of my heart. It doesn't take long for them to fall asleep. Poor guys are exhausted.

I can tell that Silas isn't asleep yet, though. I whisper, so I don't wake the others. "Silas? You good?"

His voice is rough as he answers, "I just need to feel you for a little longer."

His face is still in the crook of my neck as I say, "Silas, talk to me."

There's a choking sound as he answers, "I was the one who got to you first." His fingers against my abdomen curl into a fist as I feel my shoulder growing wet.

"Silas?" I ask, not really sure what I'm asking, but I can hear the pain in his voice. My own eyes sting in sympathy.

"You left me. Your heart stopped beating. I was the one who gave you compressions. With each compression to keep your heart beating, mine tore further apart. You wouldn't come back, no matter what I did."

The vulnerability of this man in this moment makes the tears fall. I know it took a lot for him to show me this. To let me see this side of him. I lean further into him since my hands are being held in a death grip by the others.

He continues in a choked whisper, "The sound of your heart flatlining haunts my dreams. That horrible constant beep. The blue tint to your lips is all I can see. I've never been so afraid of losing someone."

"I need you to do something for me." I know this will probably end up being uncomfortable, but he needs it.

"Anything," he whispers.

I lean forward, but his grip on me stops me from moving too far. I turn just enough to look at him. "Crawl out from behind me. Then push the button on the bed so I'm lying down flat."

He shakes his head. "No. I'm not moving."

With a smile, I say, "Please. This will help you sleep."

He gives me a measured look but does as I ask. He's surprisingly gentle as he maneuvers out from behind me and crawls off the bed Jax is lying on.

He presses the button at the edge of the bed till I'm lying prone, then he huffs out a breath and asks, "What now?"

I lift my head to look at him with a smile. "Now, crawl over the edge of the bed and lay on my chest."

"No! First off, I weigh too much to even try that. Second, if I do that, it will mess up all of the things monitoring you."

I roll my eyes. "Should we test how stubborn I am again?"

He huffs a sigh and he growls. "No." He crawls over the edge of the bed, hesitantly making his way up. He hovers over me, looking uncertain. "Are you sure?"

I lift my head up just enough to brush my lips against his. Pulling away, I look into his eyes. "I'm sure. Lie down and get some sleep."

His eyes glisten as he takes me in before nodding. He slowly lowers until his head rests between my breasts. I hear his audible sigh as he relaxes into me further.

I wish I could run my fingers through his hair, but I know Jax and Luka need the security of my touch as well, so all I can do is whisper softly to Silas. "Listen to my heart beat. Hear how strong it is. Feel each breath I take as my chest rises and falls. I'm here because you never gave up on me, Silas."

He sucks in a breath as he replies, "I could never give up on you."

"Nor I you. So sleep."

"Thank you, baby," he whispers.

"For what?"

"For loving a monster like me."

Fucking hell, I wish I could hold him right now. "You are not a monster, Silas. There is too much good in you for you to be a monster. A beast maybe, but never a monster."

His hold on me tightens as he whispers, "I don't deserve you."

"I've got to agree with Jane on this one. You deserve so much in this world. You keep saying I'm your goddess, so let me determine what you do and don't deserve."

He lets out a wet laugh and says, "As my goddess wishes. I shall bathe in your moonlight and hope to live up to the man you believe me to be."

"You already are, Silas. You just need to see what everyone else sees. Now, sleep."

He takes a deep breath as he listens to each beat of my heart. Eventually, I hear his breathing slow and feel his body mold into mine as he begins to drift off.

"I love you, my dark beast."

His voice is quiet as he replies, "I love you, my beautiful moon."

I'm lying on my hospital bed, finally able to run my fingers through Silas's hair like I wanted to last night. Jax and Luka woke up about an hour ago and went to get something to eat. Me? I think I woke up about an hour before they did. Seems when you've done nothing but sleep for a week, your body doesn't want anymore.

I look up when I hear the door to the room open. I smile as I see Jax and Luka slipping through with bacon hanging from their mouths. Jax holds up a large tray as Luka shuts the door.

They climb onto the beds they were using last night to sleep beside me. I'm still lying with Silas, who is slightly beside me now, but his head is still nestled between my breasts to hear the beating of my heart.

I'm still playing with his hair as Jax points down at him with a piece of bacon. "I'm glad he's finally resting. He hasn't slept soundly the last week."

I hum in response as I continue to play with his hair. "I remember you mentioning that he has a hard time sleeping. Mind sharing more details?"

Luka is the one who answers. "My brother holds many demons. Anger and pain have been his constant companions over the years."

Jax adds, "He's been betrayed, deceived, and hurt by too many. I've watched that man fight the grasp of the river Styx."

"The only time I have ever seen him serene is when he sees you," Luka says as he smiles down at Silas. I feel Silas shift a bit as his hold on me tightens.

"Shush, it's okay. I'm here," I whisper as I run my fingers through his hair, soothing him as I listen to his breathing.

He settles once more as he mumbles in his sleep, "I love you, little moon."

I smile as I whisper back, "I love you too. Now rest."

His grip on me loosens as his breathing slows, and his soft snores echo around the room.

Jax grins down at his brother as he says, "This is the first time I've seen him this peaceful while sleeping. Although, he hasn't really slept, so I'm sure he's exhausted."

Luka holds a piece of bacon over my face. "You want a bite, Mac?" he teases.

I smile and open my mouth. With a smirk he lowers it enough for me to take a bite. I hold back a moan at the taste. Food. Glorious food. I love bacon! So good.

I finish chewing before opening my mouth for more. Jax laughs as he holds another piece out for me. "I'm sure you're hungry, Mace."

I nod as I chew. Once I'm done, I say, "Starving, to be honest."

Jax nods as he pinches a bit of egg between his fingers, holding it over my mouth. "I'm sure. I can feed you while Prince Charming sleeps."

I snort out a laugh that makes my chest twinge in pain, but I ignore it as I say, "He's no Prince Charming. He's more like the beast from *Beauty and the Beast.*"

Jax snickers as he drops the egg into my mouth. "True enough. Does that make me Prince Charming?"

I smile. "If anyone is Prince Charming, it's Luka. You're more like the big bad wolf."

He raises a brow. "And how am I the big bad wolf?"

I grin as I say, "You would gobble me up if you had the chance."

He laughs as he moves closer to lean over me. He presses his lips softly to mine, then pulls away with a soft smile. "I know I do love all your goodies."

I chuckle softly as he sits back onto the bed. "I do love your big..."

Jax interrupts me with a laugh, "Mace!"

"I was going to say big hands. You have such a dirty mind," I tease with a laugh.

Luka chuckles as he says, "We all know you weren't going to say hands, Mac."

I grin because I can't deny it. They smile down at me as they take turns feeding me from the tray Jax brought in. They talk about random things, but I'm just happy to spend time with them. To be alive.

CHAPTER
THIRTY-EIGHT

After another long week in the medical bay at the cave, the doctor finally clears me. He said he wants me to check in with him weekly for a bit, though. At this point, I would have agreed to anything. I'm tired of being stuck inside and not being able to walk around. Plus, I have some unfinished business to attend to.

"They have been holding onto Marvin for you while you've been healing," Silas says as he helps me into my clothes. I don't need the help, but seeing this side of Silas had me caving pretty quickly when it came to letting him help.

"I'll have to give them my thanks," I comment with a smile as I let my fingers slip into his hair while he slips shoes onto my feet.

Hazel eyes meet mine as he looks up at me, and his voice is soft as he asks, "How are you feeling today, my beautiful moon?"

My fingers continue to easily slide through his beautiful strands. Moving one hand to cup his cheek, I say, "I'm doing fine, my darkest beast."

His eyes close, as I caress his cheek with my thumb, and his hands move from my feet to cup the back of my thighs. His whispered words only for the two of us. "I love you."

I smile as I bend to press my lips to his. It's brief, but I let my lips caress his for a moment before I reply, "And I love you."

Our moment is cut short when Jax and Luka enter the room. Jax looks at me with a smile. "You ready, Mace?"

I nod as I step back a bit so Silas can stand. He looks down at me before looking at his brothers. "Time to head to the dungeon."

I follow behind Silas as we exit the room that has been my home for the last week and make our way down several hallways. Jax slips his hand into mine as Luka does the same. I give them both a gentle squeeze and a smile.

We walk down a few more hallways before I see Jane standing in front of a door that I assume leads to where Marvin is being held. She turns as she hears us coming. Her belly bump is on full display now that she is in the last of her third trimester.

She smiles as she rubs her abdomen, and the two hellhounds beside her stiffen. She laughs and holds up a hand. "Down, boys. Forgive them, these boys are new."

Jax snorts beside me and says, "They seem a bit jumpy. The pups need to wet their fur a bit."

Jane laughs. "Well, my Alpha and Beta are too busy in charge of the Underground these days. I need to train some new pups to replace them."

"I find it hard to believe you could replace us with these pups, Seph." Jax snickers.

She grins. "You and Alpha are hard to replace. The pups are still learning. Your replacements are off doing their jobs. These two are only guarding the prisoner."

Silas stiffens beside me. "Who is guarding you?"

Jane raises a brow. "Do you think I need protecting?"

Silas opens his mouth, but I elbow him in the side. "Shut up, Alpha. Seph is more than capable of protecting herself."

Silas growls beside me but does as I say.

Jane snickers. "Smart woman you got there." She gestures to the door as she says, "I suppose you would like to get to it."

I stare at the door for a moment trying to gather my courage before nodding. She smiles as she makes her way over to me. When she's in front of me she smiles. "This is the same room where I got my revenge. I hope it brings you as much closure as it did me." She bends forward just enough to whisper, "Make him regret the day he was born."

God, I fucking love this woman. I give her a nod, and she gives me one in return. Gesturing over her shoulder to the two males guarding the door, she says, "Let's go boys. This door no longer needs protecting."

The two pups give us a nod before following Jane as she walks away. My eyes are still on the door as I take a deep breath before making my way toward it. Each step feels heavier than the last. Am I ready to face him?

Jax's hand still in mine gives me a gentle squeeze. "We are here with you every step of the way."

Luka squeezes my other hand. "You are not alone."

I feel Silas's breath against my neck as his hands settle on my hips. "Your wolves are here with you. Our claws and teeth are yours to command."

A shiver races down my spine as I take one last deep breath. "Then let's begin, my dark wolves."

The moment I enter the room and see his face, I know. I know that I'm ready to face him. Not only because I have my boys at my back, but also because he no longer has control over me. This pitiful broken man in front of me no longer holds my chains.

It seems that Jane's boys had some fun with him as well. My eyes roam the room, and I see a table with a variety of items on it. My eyes zero in on a knife. I smile as I make my way over without hesitation.

The metal feels surprisingly warm in my hand as I move to circle him. "Do you know why I hate men like you?" I don't let him answer as I run the tip of my knife across his cheek. Blood blooms from the small cut.

"Men like you believe the little dangling thing between your legs gives you power over women. As if you are the superior species." I slip the knife under his chin to force him look into my eyes. "But I feel like you forget that your little dangling bits are also your weakness." I grab his crotch and squeeze, and he begins to scream behind the gag.

"Men like you are NOTHING without this little thing between your legs." I squeeze harder as I say, "You are nothing but a plague on this Earth."

I release his crotch, wiping my hand on my thighs as if I could wipe his presence off me. "You forget your place in this world. A man would be nothing without a woman. You would not exist without the womb of a woman." I huff out a sigh as I continue, "Yes a woman needs sperm to create a baby, but you know we can get that from any dick."

I sneer at his crotch as I say, "*No one* needs yours, though." With that, I slam the knife into his crotch and revel in his screams that echo throughout the small room.

I look over to Silas and point to Marvin. "Quiet him, please."

Silas grins. "With pleasure, Selene." He shoves a dirty rag into Marvin's mouth, stuffing the previous gag further into his throat.

I point over to the table next and say to Jax with a grin, "Could you get me another knife?" He nods.

I turn back to Marvin as I ask Luka, "Could you hold his head back for me, Apollo?"

"Of course." Luka slips his hand through Marvin's hair. He fists it as he forces his head back to look up at me.

I grab the knife Jax offers with a smile and pat Marvin's cheek with the flat edge. Tears stream down his face as snot seeps into the makeshift gag in his mouth.

I repeat the words this man once said to me with a sickening sweet smile. "Cry for me, baby."

His breathing sounds disgusting as he tries to suck in a breath though his snotty nose. His eyes plead as he tries to talk through the gag.

I reach down, pressing harder on the knife stuck in his crotch as I growl, "I said cry for me, baby."

He chokes on a sob as tears stream down his face.

I release the pressure on the knife as I tower over him again. Tapping the other knife to his cheek, I say, "That's it. Take my knife like I had to take your disgusting cock. You're such a good little fucking whore."

I turn to Silas as I ask, "Do you have a lighter?"

He arches a brow before nodding. "Yes, why?"

I hand my new knife to him as I say, "Could you heat this for me?"

He takes the knife from me and begins to heat the metal as I turn back to Marvin. "I wouldn't want him to bleed to death before we've had our fun."

A bellowing laugh escapes Jax as Luka shakes his head with a soft chuckle.

"It's almost ready," Silas says.

"Good. I will remove the other knife, and you will press this one to the wound."

Silas gives me a look of disgust but nods. I rip out the knife currently buried in Marvin's crotch, and Silas immediately presses the molten knife to the bloody mess I made of his dick.

Muffled screams, burned flesh, and the smell of iron fill the room. They seep into my nose, and I have to admit, I've never smelled a more satisfying revenge.

CHAPTER THIRTY-NINE

MACY

"Where are you guys taking me?" I laugh as they lead me to the car while blindfolded. "Wouldn't it have been easier to blindfold me once I was in the car?"

"Now, where would the fun be in that, Mac?" Luka asks as he tugs me into the backseat.

Jax puts a hand on the top of my head, so I don't hit the door frame as I duck inside. "I know I agreed to this plan, but I don't think we completely thought this through. She has a point."

"I told you two that this was a bad idea," Silas grumbles from the front seat.

"And he's often right," I singsong.

Jax grunts and says, "Too late. We've already committed."

Adjusting myself in the seat, I feel around for the seatbelt. "You guys still haven't told me where we are going. Where could we possibly be going at ten at night?"

Luka leans across me, grabbing the seatbelt and clicking it into place. "It's a surprise."

"Can you at least give me a hint? I'm blindfolded in a moving car. If this isn't the start of a mafia kidnapping movie, I don't know what is."

Jax threads his fingers with mine as he laughs. "Kidnapping would imply that you didn't come willingly."

I hum in response. "Not the point. Si," I whine, "give me a hint."

Even though he huffs out a sigh, I can hear the smile in his voice as he says, "You mentioned that you wanted to go on a group date."

"So... we are going on a group date?"

"Yes, my moon."

"Mhm... still doesn't explain the blindfold." I point to my covered eyes for emphasis.

Luka grabs my hand and threads his fingers with mine. "It's a surprise. I promise it will be worth it."

Huffing out a sigh, I lay my head on Luka's shoulder as I sit in darkness. He did a great job with our date, so if he had anything to do with this, I'm sure it will be great. I don't realize that I fell asleep until I feel myself being gently jostled.

"It's time to wake up, Mace."

Groaning, I yawn. "I'm awake. Can I see the surprise now?"

"Almost," Luka says softly behind me as I slide across the seat. Jax takes my hand and helps me out of the car. We walk a few steps from the car before I hear Silas.

"Okay. You can remove your blindfold now." His voice sounds a bit timid, but I do as he says.

Removing my blindfold, it takes a few moments for my eyes to adjust, but when they do, I find that we are in the same spot that Luka brought me to on our first date. Though the setup is completely different. Instead of it being well lit with fairy lights and lamps, lanterns flicker softly. They give off just enough light that you can see where to walk.

A large blanket is spread out on the ground for us to lie on, and I look up into the sky to find thousands of stars twinkling above us. Laughing, I rush over to the blanket, instantly finding the best spot to lie down.

Noticing the guys haven't moved, I look in their direction. "Aren't you guys coming over to lie with me?"

Jax and Luka immediately jump into action as they rush over to the blanket. Each of them laying their heads next to mine as they lie facing the opposite direction. I pat my abdomen as I stare up at the stars. "The best spot is saved for you, Silas."

He slowly makes his way over to us and sits down. His head finds a spot on my stomach, and I slip my fingers into his hair, caressing his scalp as my fingers slide through the strands. His hair has admittedly gotten longer, which I don't mind.

He sighs, and I feel his body start to relax as I play with his hair. We lie in silence until I ask, "Have I ever mentioned that I love looking at the stars?"

Luka hums beside me. "No. I would have brought you out here more often if I had known."

I turn my head just enough to press a quick kiss to Luka's cheek. "It's alright. It's just hard to see the stars in the city."

"What do you love about them, Mace?" Jax asks softly beside me.

My mind jumps straight to my dad. My heart aches at the realization that I still haven't done anything for him. I don't realize that my fingers have stopped running through Silas's hair, until his voice pierces through my thoughts.

"Macy? Are you alright?"

Humming, I continue playing with his silky strands. "My dad... he would take me out to look at the stars when I was younger. After my mom left, it was only the two of us. He worked really hard to make ends meet for a while, and when he had a weekend off, we would go out and look at the stars."

My eyes begin to burn at the memories. "He would tell me stories about the constellations and stars themselves," I explain softly.

"What sort of stories?" Silas asks.

Huffing out a breath and trying to dismiss the sadness, I focus on the happy memories. "He would tell me stories about the constellations like

Ursa Major and Minor and the Greek mythology that went along with them. He also said that the stars sprinkled throughout the constellations are the souls of the people we have loved and lost. They are put up there so they can still watch over us."

Jax hums beside me. "I like that."

"Do you... do you think my dad is up there?"

"Without a doubt," Silas says matter-of-factly.

"How are you so sure, Si?"

He's silent for a moment before he says, "Because that would mean my brother is up there too."

"They can't all possibly be souls up there, though. What happens to the stars that are there just to shine?" Jax points out, as if there couldn't possibly be thousands of souls that become stars.

Luka points to a few of the stars in the sky as he says, "I suppose they explode like the others. They are already gone by the time we see the beauty of their shine."

I snort out a laugh. "The stars aren't gone. Just the shine."

He bumps his temple to mine as he asks, "What do you mean?"

I lift my arms up to the sky, spreading my fingers wide as if I could touch the very stars themselves. "When a star dies, it explodes into thousands of pieces, so they are always there. And, if there's a large enough explosion, it can cause the birth of a new star. So even in death, that star can be part of another star. Forever shining."

Jax hums beside me. "That doesn't sound too bad for the soul stars, either."

"Even when we are among the stars. I'll find you," Luka whispers beside me.

EPILOGUE
MACY

"Let's go!" I yell from the elevator. It's been three months since Jane had the baby, and they are finally allowing visitors. Jace called, saying that Jane has been begging for Silas and her best friend. She had apparently told him she needed to be around people other than her annoying husbands.

I clap my hands, trying to get them to hurry up. "Let's go!"

"The baby is still going to be there no matter what time we get there," Silas yells from the stairs.

"I know, but I haven't seen Jane in forever! And she's finally going to tell us the baby's name. I'm tired of calling her baby."

Jax follows behind Silas as they make their way over to the elevator. "Why are you so excited about the baby, anyways? I remember you saying you hated kids."

Rolling my eyes I say, "I don't like other people's kids. This baby does not fall into that category."

Jax laughs. "How so?"

I shrug. "She belongs to Jane." Cupping my hands around my mouth, I yell, "Luka, hurry up or we'll leave you behind!"

I watch as he rushes down the stairs and into the elevator. "Sorry, Mac." He holds up a small bag. "I almost forgot the baby gift."

I clap my hands with a squeal. "We are going to spoil her!"

"I'm sure her fathers already have that covered," Silas says as the elevator door closes.

"I'm Auntie Mace, which means I will be the awesome aunt who gets her all the things her parents won't."

As we make our way into the house, Jane greets us with a little bundle in her arms. "Hey, guys," she says softly as she adjusts the baby for us to see.

My hands cover my mouth as I gasp. "She's so beautiful," I whisper.

Jane smiles as she comes over to me. "Would you like to hold her?"

I immediately make grabby hands. "Absolutely! Give her to Auntie Mace!"

She laughs as we both adjust our holds. Jane releases her into my arms, and I look down at the small little cutie. The guys surround me, watching as I slowly rock her. "Do we finally get to know her name?"

"Her name is Silvie," Jane says softly.

My eyes immediately look to Silas. His eyes widen for a moment before they soften, and he looks down at the bundle in my arms. "Hey, Silvie."

I bite my lip before turning toward him. "The godfather should hold his goddaughter, don't you think?"

I watch as his eyes widen with fear, and he argues, "I shouldn't. She's so small."

I give him a reassuring smile. "I'll be here. Now, open your arms." He still looks panicked but does as I say. I try to coach him through the process. "Good, now, I'm going to go high, and you'll go low. My arms will slip out, and yours will take my place."

He nods as he crouches himself to put his arms where mine are. I slowly remove the arm holding her butt as he takes my place. I look up at him with a smile. "Good. Now, I'll slip my arm out from under her head, but I'll still have my hand supporting it until you have her, alright?"

Eyes still wide, he gives me a nod, and I slowly move my arms. She's fully in his arms as I take a step back. "Don't walk away!" he says in a panic.

"I'm not going anywhere, Silas. You've got this. You're doing really well. Just support her head." I give him a reassuring squeeze on his forearm. "You can stop squatting, though," I say with a laugh.

Standing to his full height now, his body is still stiff as he holds Silvie. I can hear him softly muttering beside me. "What am I doing? I shouldn't be holding a baby. She's too small. I could break her."

I begin rubbing his back as I say, "You're doing amazing, Si. Relax, I'm right here beside you."

It takes him a moment, but he eventually begins to relax and starts rocking Silvie lightly. "Hey, little one. I'm your godfather apparently, but you can call me Uncle Si."

Silvie begins to babble, and I laugh. "Seems she wants to talk to you." Her little hand reaches out toward Silas as her babbling grows louder.

Readjusting his hold, he positions a hand above hers. "She's so tiny," he says in a whisper. He gasps as her little hand grabs ahold of his finger. My eyes shift from Silvie to his face.

The panic and fear disappear from his eyes, as awe and astonishment take their place. My eyes sting when I hear his whispered words.

"There is nothing for you to fear in this life, little cub. I never thought I could love in this life..." his eyes meet mine for a moment before settling on her again. "I didn't know what love was until I met your Aunt. So know these words are truer than anything I could ever say in this lifetime. I love you, little cub."

His shining eyes meet mine again as he whispers, "I love you too, my radiant moon."

No matter what this life may bring, always know that my love surpasses even death. No matter how many lifetimes we live, I will always find and love you all over again. Even when we are nothing but dust among the stars, I will always find you.

ABOUT AUTHOR

Ivy Cole is a long time lover of writing and has wanted to publish her books for years. She love Reverse Harem of many kinds. She's a baby author and can't wait to share future books with you.
Want to follow Ivy Cole and see future books? Follow her at:
https://www.facebook.com/groups/508646927449550/

Books Also by Ivy Cole

Underground Syndicate Series:

Underworld

Why Choose Fables:

Meddling with Madness (Wonderland Retelling)

ALSO BY

<u>Books Also by Ivy Cole</u>

Underground Syndicate Series:

Underworld

Tartarus

Why Choose Fables:

Meddling with Madness (Wonderland Retelling)